U0084678

序 言

　　自「全民英檢」初級測驗實施以來，參加考試的人數逐年增加，顯示國人越來越重視這項檢定考試，因此我們陸續推出「初級英語聽力檢定①～⑥」、「初級英語模擬試題①～④」、「初級英語口說能力測驗」、「初級英語寫作能力測驗」等，以回應讀者朋友們的需求。

　　本書中所有的對話內容，均由本公司美籍老師親筆撰寫，用字遣詞最接近美國人的說法。讀者朋友做練習之餘，還可以模仿 CD 中外國人說話的語氣，大聲地朗讀出來，以熟悉各類句型的語調，增加語感，為初檢複試的「口說能力測驗」暖身。

　　本書共收錄 12 回聽力測驗，所有試題均附有詳細的中文翻譯及單字註解。在第三部份「簡短對話」中，穿插了一些較難的單字或片語，旨在培養讀者朋友依前後文來判斷字意的能力，以避免在參加考試時，聽或看到不懂的字，而慌了手腳。

　　考聽力的時候，建議讀者先看選項，再聽題目，遇到題目聽不懂時，要趕快放棄，先看下一題，絕對要超前錄音帶內容，先看選項，不能落後；此外，可能會出現三個選項都與問題相關，所以要聽清楚題目的重點，及其所使用的動詞時態；再者，要有開放的心胸，把「醫生都是男的；只有女生才會煮飯」的傳統觀念丟掉，否則它可能會擾亂讀者在第三部份「簡短（男女）對話」的作答。掌握上述原則，就可掌握得分關鍵！

　　本書是由美籍老師 Laura E. Stewart 編寫考題，蔡惠婷小姐整理資料並加上註釋，謝靜芳老師校訂，白雪嬌小姐設計封面，陳又嘉小姐繪製插圖。

劉　毅

All rights reserved. No part of this publication may be reproduced without the prior permission of Learning Publishing Company.

本書版權為學習出版公司所有，翻印必究。

全民英語能力分級檢定測驗
初級測驗①

一、聽力測驗

本測驗分三部份，全為三選一之選擇題，每部份各 10 題，共 30 題，作答時間約 20 分鐘。

第一部份：看圖辨義

本部份共 10 題，試題冊上每題有一個圖片，請聽錄音機播出一個相關的問題，與 A、B、C 三個英語敘述後，選一個與所看到圖片最相符的答案，並在答案紙上相對的圓圈內塗黑作答。每題播出一遍，問題及選項均不印在試題冊上。

例：（看）

（聽）

Look at the picture.　How much is the hamburger?

    A.　It's eighty dollars.
    B.　It's fifty-five dollars.
    C.　It's eighteen dollars.

正確答案為 A

A. **Questions 1-2**

Sean Black
#101 5th Ave
New York, NY 01234
U.S.A.

Miss. Jamie Lee
#54 Cheng Kung Road
Tainan City, Taiwan
R.O.C.

B. **Question 3**

C. **Question 4**

D. **Question 5**

請翻頁 ▯⟹

E. **Question 6**

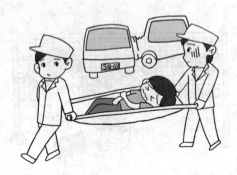

F. **Question 7**

G. **Question 8**

H. **Question 9**

I. **Question 10**

請翻頁 ▯▯▯▷

第二部份：問答

本部份共 10 題，每題錄音機會播出一個問句或直述句，每題播出一次，聽後請從試題冊上 A、B、C 三個選項中，選出一個最適合的回答或回應，並在答案紙上塗黑作答。

例：

（聽） Good morning, Kevin. How are you?

（看） A. I'm fine, thank you.
B. I'm in the living room.
C. My name is Kevin.

正確答案為 A

11. A. Yes, there's room.
B. Yes, it's in the room.
C. No, it's 201.

12. A. There are no more hangers.
B. It's not that cold today.
C. Here you are.

13. A. Here's my new business card.
B. No, I carry a mobile phone instead.
C. Yes. I often use them when I shop.

14. A. Let's pick those.
B. I can give you some seeds.
C. I like your garden, too.

15. A. Yes, it was very
       crowded with
       families.
    B. Only dogs and birds.
    C. I saw it in the tree.

16. A. Yes, we lived in the
       countryside.
    B. I was twelve years
       old.
    C. No, I was an angel.

17. A. I was splashed by the
       waterfall.
    B. I took my umbrella.
    C. It's not raining now.

18. A. I'd like some rice.
    B. Yes, please.
    C. Yes, I like them.

19. A. It went bad.
    B. I opened it.
    C. We burned it last
       night.

20. A. Sure. They were
       swimming just
       offshore.
    B. Yes, but only small
       ones.
    C. No, it wasn't too
       crowded.

請 翻 頁 ⊫⟹

第三部份：　簡短對話

　　本部份共 10 題，每題錄音機會播出一段對話及一個相關的問題，每題播出兩次，聽後請從試題冊上 A、B、C 三個選項中，選出一個最適合的回答，並在答案紙上塗黑作答。

　　例：

　　（聽）(Woman)　Good afternoon, …Mr. Davis?

　　　　 (Man)　　Yes.　I have an appointment with Dr. Sanders at two o'clock.　My son Tommy has a fever.

　　　　 (Woman)　Oh, that's too bad.　Well, please have a seat, Mr. Davis.　Dr. Sanders will be right with you.

　　　　 Question:　Where did this conversation take place?

　　（看）A.　In a post office.

　　　　 B.　In a restaurant.

　　　　 C.　In a doctor's office.

　　　　正確答案為 C

21. A. She goes by bus.
    B. She wears jeans.
    C. Her uniform.

22. A. It is very popular.
    B. It is too hot.
    C. It is broken.

23. A. She does not know how much the earrings cost.
    B. She will give the earrings to the man.
    C. The earrings were not expensive.

24. A. He will find out if he is busy on Friday.
    B. He will come to the meeting on Friday.
    C. He will schedule the next meeting.

25. A. She spent one year in England.
    B. She is British.
    C. She found England quite boring.

26. A. For five years.
    B. She has known her all her life.
    C. Since they were in elementary school.

請 翻 頁 ⫿⟹

27. A. She is both an
      American and a
      Canadian.
    B. She is their Canadian
      friend.
    C. She is a well-known
      Canadian actress.

28. A. They ran 10 kilometers.
    B. They could not run 10
      kilometers because it
      was too hard.
    C. The man doubts that
      they can run 10
      kilometers.

29. A. He will go to the
      concert with Sarah.
    B. He will ask Sarah
      to babysit.
    C. He will tell Sarah
      that he cannot go.

30. A. Her husband, her
      children and her.
    B. Her parents, her
      grandparents and
      her.
    C. Her parents, her
      brother and sister,
      and her.

初級英語聽力檢定①詳解

第一部份

For questions number 1 and 2, please look at picture A.

1. (**A**) Where does Sean Black live?

　　A. In New York.　　B. He wrote to Jamie Lee.

　　C. On Cheng Kung Road.

　　* live〔lɪv〕v. 住　New York〔nu'jɔrk〕n. 紐約
　　write to sb. 寫信給某人　road〔rod〕n. 路

2. (**C**) Please look at picture A again. What did Jamie Lee receive?

　　A. By e-mail.　　B. In Taiwan.

　　C. A letter.

　　* receive〔rɪ'siv〕v. 接到;收到
　　by〔baɪ〕prep. 藉由;用　e-mail〔'i‚mel〕n. 電子郵件

For question number 3, please look at picture B.

3. (**C**) What is she doing?

　　A. She is wearing a long-sleeved shirt.

　　B. She has a dress.　　C. She is getting dressed.

　　* wear〔wɛr〕v. 穿著
　　long-sleeved〔'lɔŋ‚slivd〕adj. 長袖的
　　shirt〔ʃɝt〕n. 襯衫　dress〔drɛs〕n. 洋裝　v. 穿衣服
　　get + **p.p.** 成為～的狀態
　　She is getting dressed. 她正在穿衣服。

For question number 4, please look at picture C.

4. (**B**) How many players are there?

　　　　A. They are playing volleyball.

　　　　B. There are five.

　　　　C. They play well.

　　　* player〔'pleɚ〕*n.* 球員

　　　　volleyball〔'vɑlɪ,bɔl〕*n.* 排球

　　　　play〔ple〕*v.* 打（球）　　well〔wɛl〕*adv.* 良好地

For question number 5, please look at picture D.

5. (**A**) How does he feel?

　　　　A. He feels full.

　　　　B. He was hungry.

　　　　C. He had dinner.

　　　* feel〔fil〕*v.* 覺得　　full〔fʊl〕*adj.* 吃飽的

　　　　hungry〔'hʌŋgrɪ〕*adj.* 飢餓的

　　　　have〔hæv〕*v.* 吃；喝　　dinner〔'dɪnɚ〕*n.* 晚餐

For question number 6, please look at picture E.

6. (**A**) How did the man get hurt?

　　　　A. There was a car accident.

　　　　B. Yes, he did.

　　　　C. He is very badly hurt.

　　　* hurt〔hɝt〕*v.* 傷害（動詞三態同形）

　　　　get hurt 受傷　　accident〔'æksədənt〕*n.* 意外

　　　　car accident 車禍　　badly〔'bædlɪ〕*adv.* 嚴重地

For question number 7, please look at picture F.

7. (**C**)　Where is the crab?

　　　　A. On top of the box.

　　　　B. In the water.

　　　　C. On the sand.

　　　* crab〔kræb〕*n.* 螃蟹　　top〔tɑp〕*n.* 頂端
　　　　sand〔sænd〕*n.* 沙子

For question number 8, please look at picture G.

8. (**A**)　What is chasing him?

　　　　A. Some angry bees.

　　　　B. Because he shot at them.

　　　　C. They are chasing the boy.

　　　* chase〔tʃes〕*v.* 追逐　　angry〔'æŋgrɪ〕*adj.* 生氣的
　　　　bee〔bi〕*n.* 蜜蜂　　because〔bɪ'kɔz〕*conj.* 因為
　　　　shoot〔ʃut〕*v.* 射擊（三態變化為：shoot-shot-shot）

For question number 9, please look at picture H.

9. (**B**)　What is she watching?

　　　　A. No, she is crying.

　　　　B. A sad TV show.

　　　　C. In the living room.

　　　* watch〔wɑtʃ〕*v.* 看
　　　　cry〔kraɪ〕*v.* 哭　　sad〔sæd〕*adj.* 悲傷的
　　　　TV show 電視節目　　*living room* 客廳

For question number 10, please look at picture I.

10. (**C**) Where is his right hand?

　　　　A. He raised his hand.

　　　　B. In the air.

　　　　C. It's under the desk.

　　　　* right〔raɪt〕*adj.* 右邊的　　hand〔hænd〕*n.* 手
　　　　　raise〔res〕*v.* 舉起　　***in the air*** 在空中
　　　　　under〔'ʌndɚ〕*prep.* 在…之下
　　　　　desk〔dɛsk〕*n.* 書桌

第二部份

11. (**C**) Is this room 101?

　　　　A. Yes, there's room.

　　　　B. Yes, it's in the room.

　　　　C. No, it's 201.

　　　　* room〔rum〕*n.* 房間；空間
　　　　　room 101 101室；101號房

12. (**A**) Why didn't you hang up your coat?

　　　　A. There are no more hangers.

　　　　B. It's not that cold today.

　　　　C. Here you are.

　　　　* ***hang up*** 掛起　　coat〔kot〕*n.* 外套
　　　　　more〔mor〕*adj.* 多餘的
　　　　　hanger〔'hæŋɚ〕*n.* 衣架；掛（衣）鉤
　　　　　It's not that cold today. 今天沒那麼冷。
　　　　　Here you are. 你要的東西在這裡；拿去吧。(= *Here it is.*)

13. (**C**) Do you have any credit cards?

    A. Here's my new business card.

    B. No, I carry a mobile phone instead.

    C. Yes. I often use them when I shop.

    * credit〔'krɛdɪt〕*n.* 信用

       credit card 信用卡   ***Here is*** ~ . 這是～。

       business card 名片

       carry〔'kærɪ〕*v.* 攜帶

       mobile〔'mobḷ〕*adj.* 可移動的

       phone〔fon〕*n.* 電話 (= *telephone*)

       mobile phone 行動電話 (= *cell phone*)

       instead〔ɪn'stɛd〕*adv.* 作爲代替

       often〔'ɔfən〕*adv.* 經常   use〔juz〕*v.* 使用

       shop〔ʃɑp〕*v.* 購物

14. (**B**) I'd like to grow some flowers in my garden.

    A. Let's pick those.

    B. I can give you some seeds.

    C. I like your garden, too.

    * ***would like to V*** . 想要 ~ (= *want to V.*)

       grow〔gro〕*v.* 種植

       flower〔'flauɚ〕*n.* 花   garden〔'gɑrdn̩〕*n.* 花園

       pick〔pɪk〕*v.* 挑選   give〔gɪv〕*v.* 給

       seed〔sid〕*n.* 種子

15. (**B**) Did you see any animals in the park?

    A. Yes, it was very crowded with families.

    B. Only dogs and birds.

    C. I saw it in the tree.

    * animal〔'ænəml̩〕n. 動物

      park〔pɑrk〕n. 公園

      crowded〔'kraʊdɪd〕adj. 擁擠的

16. (**C**) Were you naughty when you were a child?

    A. Yes, we lived in the countryside.

    B. I was twelve years old.

    C. No, I was an angel.

    * naughty〔'nɔtɪ〕adj. 頑皮的

      child〔tʃaɪld〕n. 小孩（複數形為 children）

      countryside〔'kʌntrɪ,saɪd〕n. 鄉村地區

      ~years old ~歲

      angel〔'endʒəl〕n. 天使；乖巧的小孩

17. (**A**) How did you get so wet?

    A. I was splashed by the waterfall.

    B. I took my umbrella.

    C. It's not raining now.

    * get〔gɛt〕v. 變得　　so〔so〕adv. 如此地

      wet〔wɛt〕adj. 濕的　　splash〔splæʃ〕v.（水）飛濺

      waterfall〔'wɔtɚ,fɔl〕n. 瀑布　　take〔tek〕v. 拿

      umbrella〔ʌm'brɛlə〕n. 雨傘　　rain〔ren〕v. 下雨

18. (**A**) Would you prefer rice or noodles?

    A. I'd like some rice.

    B. Yes, please.

    C. Yes, I like them.

    * prefer〔prɪ'fɝ〕v. 比較喜歡

      rice〔raɪs〕n. 米飯   noodle〔'nudḷ〕n. 麵

      would like 想要（= *want*）

19. (**C**) What happened to the candle?

    A. It went bad.

    B. I opened it.

    C. We burned it last night.

    * ***happen to*** … 發生在…身上

      candle〔'kændḷ〕n. 蠟燭

      go〔go〕v. 變成（不好的狀況）

      go bad （食物）變壞   open〔'opən〕v. 打開

      burn〔bɝn〕v. 燃燒   ***last night*** 昨晚

20. (**B**) Were there any waves at the beach?

    A. Sure. They were swimming just offshore.

    B. Yes, but only small ones.

    C. No, it wasn't too crowded.

    * wave〔wev〕n. 海浪   beach〔bitʃ〕n. 海邊

      sure〔ʃur〕adv. 當然   swim〔swɪm〕v. 游泳

      just〔dʒʌst〕adv. 就在

      offshore〔'ɔf'ʃor〕adv. 在近海處

      ones 代替前面提及的複數名詞，在此指 waves「海浪」。

第三部份

21. (**C**) M: Do you ever wear jeans to school?

W: No. We're not allowed to.

M: Why not?

W: We have uniforms.

Question: What does the woman usually wear to school?

A. She goes by bus.　　B. She wears jeans.

C. Her uniform.

* ever〔'ɛvɚ〕*adv.* 曾經　　wear〔wɛr〕*v.* 穿
jeans〔dʒinz〕*n. pl.* 牛仔褲
allow〔ə'lau〕*v.* 允許　　***Why not?*** 爲什麼不？
uniform〔'junə,fɔrm〕*n.* 制服
usually〔'juʒʊəlɪ〕*adv.* 通常　　***by bus*** 搭公車

22. (**B**) M: Has the air conditioner been repaired?

W: Not yet.

M: Then we'll need some fans for the classroom.

Question: What is the classroom like?

A. It is very popular.　　B. It is too hot.

C. It is broken.

* ***air conditioner*** 空調；冷氣機　　repair〔rɪ'pɛr〕*v.* 修理
Not yet. 還沒。　　then〔ðɛn〕*adv.* 那麼
need〔nid〕*v.* 需要　　fan〔fæn〕*n.* 風扇
like〔laɪk〕*prep.* 像　　popular〔'pɑpjəlɚ〕*adj.* 受歡迎的
hot〔hɑt〕*adj.* 熱的　　broken〔'brokən〕*adj.* 故障的

23. (**A**) M: Those are nice earrings.

W: Thank you.

M: Were they expensive?

W: They were a gift.

Question: What does the woman mean?

A. She does not know how much the earrings cost.

B. She will give the earrings to the man.

C. The earrings were not expensive.

* nice〔naɪs〕adj. 漂亮的　　earrings〔'ɪr,rɪŋz〕n. pl. 耳環
expensive〔ɪk'spɛnsɪv〕adj. 昂貴的　　gift〔gɪft〕n. 禮物
mean〔min〕v. 意思是　　cost〔kɔst〕v. 值～（錢）

24. (**A**) M: When is the next club meeting?

W: It's on Friday.　Can you make it?

M: I'll check my schedule.

Question: What does the man mean?

A. He will find out if he is busy on Friday.

B. He will come to the meeting on Friday.

C. He will schedule the next meeting.

* next〔nɛkst〕adj. 下一個　　club〔klʌb〕n. 社團
meeting〔'mitɪŋ〕n. 會議　　*make it* 能來；成功；辦到
Can you make it? 你能來嗎？
check〔tʃɛk〕v. 檢查；核對
schedule〔'skɛdʒul〕n. 行程表　v. 排定
find out 查出　　busy〔'bɪzɪ〕adj. 忙碌的
if〔ɪf〕conj. 是否

25. (**B**)   M : Have you ever been to England?

W : That's where I was born.

M : Oh! And how long has it been since you were home?

W : Over a year now.

Question : What is true about the woman?

A. She spent one year in England.

B. She is British.

C. She found England quite boring.

* **have ever been to** ~   曾經去過~

England〔'ɪŋglənd〕*n.* 英國

born〔bɔrn〕*adj.* 出生的

That's where I was born. 那是我出生的地方。

oh〔o〕*interj.* 喔（因驚訝所發出的感嘆）

since〔sɪns〕*conj.* 自從   **how long ~?** ~多久？

And how long has it been since you were home?

那從你上次回家到現在多久了？

over〔'ovɚ〕*prep.* 超過（= *more than*）

true〔tru〕*adj.* 正確的

spend〔spɛnd〕*v.* 度過（時間）

British〔'brɪtɪʃ〕*adj.* 英國人的

find〔faɪnd〕*v.* 覺得   quite〔kwaɪt〕*adv.* 非常

boring〔'borɪŋ〕*adj.* 無聊的

26. (**C**)　M：How long have you known Dana?

　　　　W：We were classmates in the fifth grade.

　　　　M：And you've kept in touch all this time?

　　　　W：Yes, we have.

　　　Question：How long has the woman known Dana?

　　　A.　For five years.

　　　B.　She has known her all her life.

　　　C.　Since they were in elementary school.

　　　* **How long ～?** ～多久？
　　　　know〔no〕v. 知道；認識
　　　　grade〔gred〕n. 年級　　**fifth grade** 五年級
　　　　keep〔kip〕v. 保持　　touch〔tʌtʃ〕n. 聯絡
　　　　keep in touch 保持聯絡
　　　　all this time 這整個期間
　　　　for〔fɔr〕prep. 持續～
　　　　all one's life 一輩子（= in one's life）
　　　　since〔sɪns〕conj. 自從
　　　　elementary〔͵ɛlə'mɛntərɪ〕adj. 初等的
　　　　elementary school 小學

27. (**B**)　M：I thought Clare was American.

　　　　W：Isn't she?

　　　　M：No.　Actually, she is Canadian.

　　　　W：I didn't know that.

　　　Question：What is true about Clare?

A. She is both an American and a Canadian.

B. She is their Canadian friend.

C. She is a well-known Canadian actress.

* think〔θɪŋk〕v. 認為（三態變化為：think-thought-thought）
American〔ə'mɛrɪkən〕adj. 美國人的　n. 美國人
actually〔'æktʃʊəlɪ〕adv. 事實上
Canadian〔kə'nedɪən〕adj. 加拿大人的　n. 加拿大人
well-known〔'wɛl'non〕adj. 有名的（= famous）
actress〔'æktrɪs〕n. 女演員

28.（**A**）M：I can hardly believe we ran 10 kilometers!

W：Didn't you think we would make it?

M：I had my doubts.

Question：What did they do?

A. They ran 10 kilometers.

B. They could not run 10 kilometers because it was
too hard.

C. The man doubts that they can run 10 kilometers.

* hardly〔'hɑrdlɪ〕adv. 幾乎不
believe〔bɪ'liv〕v. 相信　run〔rʌn〕v. 跑
kilometer〔'kɪlə,mitɚ〕n. 公里
make it 成功；辦成
doubts〔daʊts〕n. pl. 懷疑　v. 懷疑
I had my doubts. 我之前不相信。（因 had 為過去式，故
翻譯時應加上「之前」，句意會較清楚。）
hard〔hɑrd〕adj. 困難的

29. (**C**) M：I got a message from Sarah.

W：What did she say?

M：She wants to know if we can go to the concert tonight.

W：We can't. I couldn't get a babysitter.

M：Okay. I'll let Sarah know.

Question：What will the man do?

A. He will go to the concert with Sarah.

B. He will ask Sarah to babysit.

C. He will tell Sarah that he cannot go.

* get〔gɛt〕v. 得到

message〔'mɛsɪdʒ〕n. 信息；留言

concert〔'kɑnsɝt〕n. 音樂會

babysitter〔'bebɪ,sɪtɚ〕n. 臨時保姆 (= baby-sitter)

okay〔'o'ke〕adv. 好 (= OK)

ask〔æsk〕v. 問；請求

babysit〔'bebɪ,sɪt〕v. 當臨時保姆 (= baby-sit)

30. (**B**) M：How many people live in your house?

W：Five.

M：You have a big family.

W：In fact, I am an only child, but there are three generations living in my house.

Question：Who lives in the woman's house?

A. Her husband, her children and her.

B. Her parents, her grandparents and her.

C. Her parents, her brother and sister, and her.

* ***in fact*** 事實上　　***only child*** 獨子
generation〔͵dʒɛnəˋreʃən〕*n.* 世代
husband〔ˋhʌzbənd〕*n.* 丈夫
children〔ˋtʃɪldrən〕*n. pl.* 小孩（child 的複數形）
parents〔ˋpɛrənts〕*n. pl.* 父母
grandparents〔ˋgrænd͵pɛrənts〕*n. pl.* 祖父母
brother〔ˋbrʌðə〕*n.* 兄弟
sister〔ˋsɪstə〕*n.* 姊妹

全民英語能力分級檢定測驗
初級測驗②

一、聽力測驗

本測驗分三部份，全為三選一之選擇題，每部份各 10 題，共 30 題，作答時間約 20 分鐘。

第一部份：看圖辨義

本部份共 10 題，試題冊上每題有一個圖片，請聽錄音機播出一個相關的問題，與 A、B、C 三個英語敘述後，選一個與所看到圖片最相符的答案，並在答案紙上相對的圓圈內塗黑作答。每題播出一遍，問題及選項均不印在試題冊上。

例：（看）

NT$80   NT$50

（聽）

Look at the picture. How much is the hamburger?

   A. It's eighty dollars.

   B. It's fifty-five dollars.

   C. It's eighteen dollars.

正確答案為 A

A. **Question 1**

B. **Question 2**

C. **Question 3**

D. <u>Question 4</u>

E. <u>Question 5</u>

F. Questions 6-7

G. <u>Question 8</u>

H. <u>Question 9</u>

I. <u>Question 10</u>

請翻頁 ▯▯⟹

第二部份：問答

本部份共 10 題，每題錄音機會播出一個問句或直述句，每題播出一次，聽後請從試題冊上 A、B、C 三個選項中，選出一個最適合的回答或回應，並在答案紙上塗黑作答。

例：

（聽） Good morning, Kevin. How are you?

（看） A. I'm fine, thank you.
B. I'm in the living room.
C. My name is Kevin.

正確答案為 A

11. A. Yes, it grows in Taiwan.
B. Okay. Let's get a can of pineapple.
C. Yeah. Those tangerines look good.

12. A. No. We have a DVD player.
B. Yes, but if it's not too hot I use a fan.
C. Sure. Do you want to go online?

13. A. Yes. He likes to go out.

    B. I don't take him out every afternoon.

    C. I left the gate open.

14. A. No, I don't need glasses.

    B. I just got contact lenses.

    C. Over there on the desk.

15. A. Put them in the dryer, please.

    B. You should have taken an umbrella.

    C. Leave them outside with the other shoes.

16. A. Don't worry. You'll find it.

    B. No, I didn't lose it.

    C. Better luck next time.

17. A. I'll stop knocking.

    B. Go see who it is.

    C. Okay. I'll close it.

18. A. I'd like to lose some weight from my waist.

    B. It's on Baker Street.

    C. No, it's quite mountainous.

19. A. I like yellow best.

    B. It's a medium.

    C. It's blue and gray.

20. A. No thanks. I know how to get there.

    B. Thanks. I'll wait here.

    C. Yes, you're in the right office.

請 翻 頁 ⫸

第三部份： 簡短對話

本部份共 10 題，每題錄音機會播出一段對話及一個相關的問題，每題播出兩次，聽後請從試題冊上 A、B、C 三個選項中，選出一個最適合的回答，並在答案紙上塗黑作答。

例：

(聽) (Woman) Good afternoon, ...Mr. Davis?

(Man) Yes. I have an appointment with Dr. Sanders at two o'clock. My son Tommy has a fever.

(Woman) Oh, that's too bad. Well, please have a seat, Mr. Davis. Dr. Sanders will be right with you.

Question: Where did this conversation take place?

(看) A. In a post office.

B. In a restaurant.

C. In a doctor's office.

正確答案為 C

21. A. It is beside the woman.

B. It is next to the street.

C. It has been stolen.

22. A. It has not been cut.

B. It has been there too long.

C. It is unemployed.

23. A. They are not so great.

    B. It is impolite.

    C. She is not really
    hungry.

24. A. She made a cake.

    B. She made a home.

    C. She made a decision.

25. A. Modern art.

    B. Cooking.

    C. History.

26. A. It is on the house.

    B. It is broken.

    C. It broke a window.

27. A. No, it was a gift.

    B. No, it is for sale.

    C. No, it is a copy.

28. A. To a city parking lot.

    B. To a nearby park.

    C. To a large park.

29. A. His favorite player
    changed teams.

    B. The Giants played
    badly.

    C. He does not support
    the Giants.

30. A. The fence was not
    strong enough to
    keep out the rabbits.

    B. The rabbits were able
    to jump over the
    fence.

    C. The rabbits cannot
    get out of the garden.

請 翻 頁 ⫸

初級英語聽力檢定 ② 詳解

第一部份

For question number 1, please look at picture A.

1. (**B**) What is wrong with the soup?

    A. It's a cockroach.

    B. There is a cockroach in it.

    C. It's the wrong soup.

    * ***What's wrong with~?*** ~怎麼了？

        (= *What's the matter with~?*)   soup〔sup〕*n.* 湯

        cockroach〔'kɑk,rotʃ〕*n.* 蟑螂 (= *roach*)

        wrong〔rɔŋ〕*adj.* 錯誤的；不對的

For question number 2, please look at picture B.

2. (**C**) What is the little girl doing?

    A. She is hungry.   B. She is shopping.

    C. She is pointing.

    * hungry〔'hʌŋgrɪ〕*adj.* 飢餓的

        shop〔ʃɑp〕*v.* 購物   point〔pɔɪnt〕*v.* 用手指

For question number 3, please look at picture C.

3. (**C**) What is in the box?

    A. A magic trick.   B. A magician.

    C. A boy.

    * magic〔'mædʒɪk〕*adj.* 魔術的   trick〔trɪk〕*n.* 把戲

        magician〔mə'dʒɪʃən〕*n.* 魔術師

For question number 4, please look at picture D.

4. (**B**) Where was the wallet?

  A. He is losing it. B. In his pocket.

  C. In the air.

  * wallet〔'walıt〕*n.* 皮夾 lose〔luz〕*v.* 遺失

   pocket〔'pakıt〕*n.* 口袋 *in the air* 在空中

For question number 5, please look at picture E.

5. (**A**) Does the boy like vegetables?

  A. No, he doesn't.

  B. Yes, he has to eat the onions.

  C. They are good for him.

  * like〔laık〕*v.* 喜歡 vegetable〔'vɛdʒətəbl̩〕*n.* 蔬菜

   onion〔'ʌnjən〕*n.* 洋蔥 good〔gʊd〕*adj.* 有益的

For question number 6 and 7, please look at picture F.

6. (**A**) Which national park is in eastern Taiwan?

  A. Toroko National Park.

  B. Yangmingshan.

  C. Yes, it is.

  * which〔hwıtʃ〕*adj.* 哪一個

   national〔'næʃənl̩〕*adj.* 國立的；國家的

   national park 國家公園 eastern〔'istən〕*adj.* 東方的

   Taiwan〔'taı'wɑn〕*n.* 台灣

   Toroko National Park 太魯閣國家公園

   Yangmingshan 陽明山

7. (**C**) Please look at picture F again.　In which county is Sun Moon Lake?
　　　A. Taiwan.　　　　B. The middle.
　　　C. Nantou.

　　　* county (′kaʊntɪ) *n.* 縣　　*Sun Moon Lake* 日月潭
　　　middle (′mɪdḷ) *n.* 中間　　*Nantou* 南投

For question number 8, please look at picture G.

8. (**C**) What is he doing in front of the TV?
　　　A. Yes, he is.　　　　B. A desk.
　　　C. His homework.

　　　* *in front of* ~ 在~前面
　　　homework (′hom‚wɝk) *n.* 家庭作業

For question number 9, please look at picture H.

9. (**B**) Where is he?
　　　A. He can swim.　　　B. At the beach.
　　　C. He is a swimming teacher.

　　　* swim (swɪm) *v.* 游泳　　beach (bitʃ) *n.* 海邊
　　　swimming (′swɪmɪŋ) *n.* 游泳

For question number 10, please look at picture I.

10. (**B**) What did the boy order?
　　　A. He does not have enough money.
　　　B. Fast food.　　　C. He lost it.

　　　* order (′ɔrdə) *v.* 點（菜）
　　　enough (ə′nʌf) *adj.* 足夠的　　*fast food* 速食

第二部份

11. (**C**) Do you want to buy some fresh fruit?

    A. Yes, it grows in Taiwan.

    B. Okay. Let's get a can of pineapple.

    C. Yeah. Those tangerines look good.

    * buy〔baɪ〕*v.* 買（三態變化為：buy-bought-bought）
    fresh〔frɛʃ〕*adj.* 新鮮的　　fruit〔frut〕*n.* 水果
    grow〔gro〕*v.* 種植；生長
    okay〔'o'ke〕*adv.* 好（= *OK*）　　***a can of*~** 一罐~
    pineapple〔'paɪn,æpl̩〕*n.* 鳳梨
    yeah〔jæ〕*adv.* 是的（= *yes*）
    tangerine〔,tændʒə'rin〕*n.* 橘子
    look good 看起來不錯

12. (**A**) Do you have a VCR at home?

    A. No. We have a DVD player.

    B. Yes, but if it's not too hot I use a fan.

    C. Sure. Do you want to go online?

    * ***VCR*** 錄影機（= *video cassette recorder*）
    DVD 數位影音光碟（= *digital video disk*）
    player〔'pleɚ〕*n.* 播放機　　hot〔hɑt〕*adj.* 熱的
    use〔juz〕*v.* 使用　　fan〔fæn〕*n.* 風扇
    sure〔ʃur〕*adv.* 當然
    online〔'ɑn,laɪn〕*adv.* 線上地；在網路上（= *on-line*）
    go online 上網

13. (**C**) How did the dog get out?

    A. Yes. He likes to go out.

    B. I don't take him out every afternoon.

    C. I left the gate open.

    * ***get out*** 出去   ***take ~out*** 帶~出去

    leave〔liv〕*v.* 使（人、物）處於（某種狀態）

    gate〔get〕*n.* 大門   open〔'opən〕*adj.* 開著的

14. (**B**) Why aren't you wearing your glasses?

    A. No, I don't need glasses.

    B. I just got contact lenses.

    C. Over there on the desk.

    * wear〔wɛr〕*v.* 戴；穿   glasses〔'glæsɪz〕*n. pl.* 眼鏡

    need〔nid〕*v.* 需要   just〔dʒʌst〕*adv.* 才；剛剛

    get〔gɛt〕*v.* 買   contact〔'kɑntækt〕*adj.* 接觸的

    lens〔lɛnz〕*n.* 鏡片   ***contact lenses*** 隱形眼鏡

    over there 在那裡

15. (**A**) What should I do with these wet towels?

    A. Put them in the dryer, please.

    B. You should have taken an umbrella.

    C. Leave them outside with the other shoes.

    * should〔ʃud〕*aux.* 應該   wet〔wɛt〕*adj.* 濕的

    towel〔'tauəl〕*n.* 毛巾   put〔put〕*v.* 放

    dryer〔'draɪɚ〕*n.* 烘乾機   ***should have + p.p.*** 早該~

    take〔tek〕*v.* 帶   umbrella〔ʌm'brɛlə〕*n.* 雨傘

    outside〔'aut'saɪd〕*adv.* 在外面

    shoes〔ʃuz〕*n. pl.* 鞋子

16. (**C**) We were the losers in yesterday's game.

A. Don't worry. You'll find it.

B. No, I didn't lose it.

C. Better luck next time.

* loser ('luzə) *n.* 失敗者　　 game (gem) *n.* 比賽

worry ('wɜɪ) *v.* 擔心　　 find (faɪnd) *v.* 找到

lose (luz) *v.* 遺失　　 better ('bɛtə) *adj.* 比較好的

luck (lʌk) *n.* 運氣

Better luck next time. 祝下次好運。

17. (**B**) Someone is knocking at the door.

A. I'll stop knocking.

B. Go see who it is.

C. Okay. I'll close it.

* someone ('sʌm,wʌn) *pron.* 某人

knock (nɑk) *v.* 敲　　 ***stop + V-ing*** 停止~

go see 去看看 (*= go to see = go and see*)

close (kloz) *v.* 關上

18. (**B**) Where is your flat?

A. I'd like to lose some weight from my waist.

B. It's on Baker Street.

C. No, it's quite mountainous.

* flat (flæt) *n.* 公寓 (*= apartment*)

would like to V. 想要 (*= want to V.*)

weight (wet) *n.* 體重　　 ***lose weight*** 減肥

waist (west) *n.* 腰　　 quite (kwaɪt) *adv.* 非常

mountainous ('maʊntn̩əs) *adj.* 多山的

19. (**C**) What color is your uniform?

    A. I like yellow best.

    B. It's a medium.

    C. It's blue and gray.

    * color〔'kʌlɚ〕*n.* 顏色
      uniform〔'junə,fɔrm〕*n.* 制服
      like…(the) best 最喜歡⋯   yellow〔'jɛlo〕*n.* 黃色
      medium〔'midɪən〕*n.* 中號的衣服
      blue〔blu〕*n.* 藍色
      gray〔gre〕*n.* 灰色（= *grey*）

20. (**A**) Would you like me to guide you to the right office?

    A. No thanks. I know how to get there.

    B. Thanks. I'll wait here.

    C. Yes, you're in the right office.

    * guide〔gaɪd〕*v.* 引導   right〔raɪt〕*adj.* 正確的
      office〔'ɔfɪs〕*n.* 辦公室   get〔gɛt〕*v.* 去到
      there〔ðɛr〕*adv.* 那裡   wait〔wet〕*v.* 等待
      here〔hɪr〕*adv.* 在這裡

第三部份

21. (**B**) M：Where did you leave your bicycle?

    W：It's on the sidewalk.

    M：You'd better lock it. Someone might steal it.

    Question：Where is the bicycle?

A. It is beside the woman.

B. It is next to the street.

C. It has been stolen.

* leave〔liv〕v. 遺留　　bicycle〔'baɪsɪk!〕n. 腳踏車
  sidewalk〔'saɪd,wɔk〕n. 人行道
  had better V. 最好～（表提議）　　lock〔lɑk〕v. 鎖
  steal〔stil〕v. 偷（三態變化爲：steal-stole-stolen）
  might〔maɪt〕aux. 可能　　　**next to**… 在…旁邊
  street〔strit〕n. 街道

22. (**A**) M: The grass looks long.

W: It does. I guess no one cut it this week.

M: Who is supposed to do that?

W: A city employee.

Question: What is wrong with the grass?

A. It has not been cut.

B. It has been there too long.

C. It is unemployed.

* grass〔græs〕n. 草　　look〔luk〕v. 看起來
  long〔lɔŋ〕adj. 長的；久的
  guess〔gɛs〕v. 猜想；認爲
  cut〔kʌt〕v. 割　　**be supposed to V.** 應該～
  city〔'sɪtɪ〕n. 城市　　employee〔ɛmplɔɪ'i〕n. 雇員
  city employee （市政府）公務人員
  unemployed〔,ʌnɪm'plɔɪd〕adj. 失業的

23. (**B**) M: Don't eat all the doughnuts.

W: Why not? I'm hungry.

M: It's so greedy.

Question: Why shouldn't the woman eat all the doughnuts?

A. They are not so great.

B. It is impolite.

C. She is not really hungry.

* doughnut〔'do,nʌt〕 *n.* 甜甜圈 (= *donut*)

Why not? 為什麼不行？

hungry〔'hʌŋgrɪ〕 *adj.* 飢餓的

so〔so〕 *adv.* 如此地

greedy〔'gridɪ〕 *adj.* 貪心的

great〔gret〕 *adj.* 很棒的

impolite〔,ɪmpə'laɪt〕 *adj.* 無禮的

really〔'rɪəlɪ〕 *adv.* 真正地

24. (**C**) M: Have you made a decision yet?

W: Yes. I think we should order one from the bakery.

M: But homemade cakes are so much nicer.

W: I know. But I don't have the time.

Question: What did the woman make?

A. She made a cake.

B. She made a home.

C. She made a decision.

* decision〔dɪˈsɪdʒən〕n. 決定　　***make a decision*** 做決定
yet〔jɛt〕adv. 已經（用於疑問句）
think〔θɪŋk〕v. 認為（三態變化為：think-thought-thought）
order〔ˈɔrdɚ〕v. 點（菜）　　bakery〔ˈbekərɪ〕n. 麵包店
homemade〔ˈhomˈmed〕adj. 自製的
cake〔kek〕n. 蛋糕　　make〔mek〕v. 做；製作

25. (**C**)　M：What did you like best in the museum?

W：I liked the ancient tools, weapons, bowls and so on.

M：Not me. I liked the modern paintings.

Question：What is the woman most likely interested in?

A. Modern art.　　　B. Cooking.

C. History.

* museum〔mjuˈziəm〕n. 博物館
ancient〔ˈenʃənt〕adj. 古老的　　tool〔tul〕n. 工具
weapon〔ˈwɛpən〕n. 武器　　bowl〔bol〕n. 碗
…and so on …等等　　modern〔ˈmadɚn〕adj. 現代的
painting〔ˈpentɪŋ〕n. 畫　　most〔most〕adv. 最～
likely〔ˈlaɪklɪ〕adj. 可能的
interested〔ˈɪntrɪstɪd〕adj. 感興趣的　　art〔art〕n. 藝術
cooking〔ˈkʊkɪŋ〕n. 烹調　　history〔ˈhɪstrɪ〕n. 歷史

26. (**A**)　M：Where is the Frisbee?

W：It's on the roof.

M：How did that happen?

W：I threw it too hard.

Question：Where is the Frisbee?

A. It is on the house.　　B. It is broken.

C. It broke a window.

* Frisbee〔'frɪzbi〕*n.* 飛盤　　roof〔ruf〕*n.* 屋頂
happen〔'hæpən〕*v.* 發生
throw〔θro〕*v.* 丟　　hard〔hɑrd〕*adv.* 用力地
broken〔'brokən〕*adj.* 故障的；壞了的
break〔brek〕*v.* 打破（三態變化爲：break-broke-broken）
window〔'wɪndo〕*n.* 窗戶

27. (**C**)　M：Is this painting valuable?

W：No, it's not an original.

M：Where did you get it?

W：At a gift store.

Question：Is the painting valuable?

A. No, it was a gift.

B. No, it is for sale.

C. No, it is a copy.

* valuable〔'væljəbl̩〕*adj.* 珍貴的
original〔ə'rɪdʒənl̩〕*n.* 原作品　　get〔gɛt〕*v.* 買
gift〔gɪft〕*n.* 禮物　　store〔stor〕*n.* 商店
for sale 出售　　copy〔'kɑpɪ〕*n.* 複製品

28. (**B**)　M：Where do you walk your dog?

W：I take him to the park.

M：The city park?

W：No, the local park.

Question：Where does the woman take the dog?

A. To a city parking lot.

B. To a nearby park.

C. To a large park.

* walk〔wɔk〕v. 遛（狗）　　take〔tek〕v. 把…帶去
park〔pɑrk〕n. 公園　v. 停車
city〔'sɪtɪ〕adj. 市立的；市的　　*city park* 市公園
local〔'lokḷ〕adj. 當地的　　*parking lot* 停車場
nearby〔'nɪr͵baɪ〕adj. 附近的
large〔lɑrdʒ〕adj. 大的

29.（**C**）M：How was the game?

W：Victory went to the Giants.

M：Oh, that's too bad.

Question：Why is the man sad?

A. His favorite player changed teams.

B. The Giants played badly.

C. He does not support the Giants.

* game〔gem〕n. 比賽　　victory〔'vɪktrɪ〕n. 勝利
go to …　（物）落入…手中
giants〔'dʒaɪənts〕n. pl. 巨人（在此表「巨人隊」）
oh〔o〕interj. 喔（因驚訝、痛苦等所發出的感嘆）
That's too bad. 真糟糕。　　sad〔sæd〕adj. 悲傷的
favorite〔'fevərɪt〕adj. 最喜愛的
player〔'pleɚ〕n. 球員　　change〔tʃendʒ〕v. 改變
team〔tim〕n. 隊　　play〔ple〕v. 打（球）
badly〔'bædlɪ〕adv. 拙劣地　　support〔sə'port〕v. 支持

30. (**B**) M: Why do you have a fence around your garden?

W: I want to keep out the rabbits.

M: I think you need a higher fence.

Question: What probably happened?

A. The fence was not strong enough to keep out the rabbits.

B. The rabbits were able to jump over the fence.

C. The rabbits cannot get out of the garden.

* fence〔fɛns〕 *n.* 籬笆   around〔ə'raʊnd〕 *prep.* 圍著

garden〔'gɑrdn̩〕 *n.* 花園

keep out 使留在外面；使不進入

rabbit〔'ræbɪt〕 *n.* 兔子

think〔θɪŋk〕 *v.* 認為（三態變化為：think-thought- thought）

need〔nid〕 *v.* 需要

higher〔'haɪɚ〕 *adj.* 較高的（high 的比較級）

probably〔'prɑbəblɪ〕 *adv.* 可能

happen〔'hæpən〕 *v.* 發生

strong〔strɔŋ〕 *adj.* 強壯的

enough〔ə'nʌf〕 *adv.* 足夠地   **be able to V.** 能夠…

jump over 跳過   **get out of…** 從…出來

全民英語能力分級檢定測驗
初級測驗③

一、聽力測驗

本測驗分三部份，全爲三選一之選擇題，每部份各 10 題，共 30 題，作答時間約 20 分鐘。

第一部份：看圖辨義

本部份共 10 題，試題冊上每題有一個圖片，請聽錄音機播出一個相關的問題，與 A、B、C 三個英語敘述後，選一個與所看到圖片最相符的答案，並在答案紙上相對的圓圈內塗黑作答。每題播出一遍，問題及選項均不印在試題冊上。

例：（看）

（聽）

Look at the picture.   How much is the hamburger?

   A.   It's eighty dollars.
   B.   It's fifty-five dollars.
   C.   It's eighteen dollars.

正確答案爲 A

Question 1

Question 2

Question 3

Question 4

Question 5

Question 6

請翻頁 ▯▭▭⇨

Question 7

Question 8

Question 9

Question 10

請翻頁 ⟹

第二部份：問答

本部份共 10 題，每題錄音機會播出一個問句或直述句，每題播出一次，聽後請從試題冊上 A、B、C 三個選項中，選出一個最適合的回答或回應，並在答案紙上塗黑作答。

例：

（聽） Good morning, Kevin. How are you?

（看） A. I'm fine, thank you.
　　　 B. I'm in the living room.
　　　 C. My name is Kevin.

正確答案爲 A

11. A. It's NT$150 per slice.
　　 B. It's an apple pie.
　　 C. There is only a quarter left.

12. A. No, I think he's in good shape.
　　 B. No, he's not married.
　　 C. No, you're not.

13. A. I took the number 86 bus.
　　 B. Yes. I went yesterday.
　　 C. I got the last copy of the *Harry Potter* book.

14. A. Yes, it's nice.
　　 B. W–I–L–L–I–A–M
　　 C. I got an A.

15. A. Yes, it's open.
    B. It's on the north side.
    C. The phone number is 2189-6707.

16. A. Yes, I did.
    B. Okay. I'll meet you there.
    C. I'd be delighted.

17. A. Yes. It was terrible.
    B. Yes, I was.
    C. No, I can't.

18. A. The sofa will be delivered tomorrow.
    B. No wonder it's so hot.
    C. That's because they are away on vacation.

19. A. No, I didn't.
    B. No. It was the doorbell.
    C. Yes, I called you yesterday.

20. A. A truck driver.
    B. It was a red light.
    C. No one was hurt.

請 翻 頁 ⟹

第三部份: 簡短對話

本部份共 10 題,每題錄音機會播出一段對話及一個相關的問題,每題播出兩次,聽後請從試題冊上 A、B、C 三個選項中,選出一個最適合的回答,並在答案紙上塗黑作答。

例:

(聽) (Woman) Good afternoon, …Mr. Davis?

(Man) Yes. I have an appointment with Dr. Sanders at two o'clock. My son Tommy has a fever.

(Woman) Oh, that's too bad. Well, please have a seat, Mr. Davis. Dr. Sanders will be right with you.

Question: Where did this conversation take place?

(看) A. In a post office.
B. In a restaurant.
C. In a doctor's office.

正確答案為 C

21. A. The chair has
      disappeared.
   B. The purse left.
   C. The purse is missing.

22. A. There is not enough
      room.
   B. The Frisbee is too
      small.
   C. They cannot go
      outside.

23. A. The local bookstore
      does not sell them.
   B. It is cheaper than
      buying them at the
      bookstore.
   C. He can buy things
      online at any time.

24. A. It refuses to exercise.
   B. It might escape
      through a window.
   C. It might make the
      house dirty.

25. A. She wants to exercise
      after lunch.
   B. The cafeteria is full of
      people at lunchtime.
   C. Eating lunch early
      is fashionable.

26. A. Yes, he sleeps during
      the break time.
   B. Yes, he often sleeps
      during class.
   C. No, he usually studies
      instead.

請 翻 頁 ▯⟹

27. A. He needs energy to
    fix the freezer.
  B. He has a cold.
  C. He is afraid the food
    will melt.

28. A. She has never been
    on a ship before.
  B. She has never taken
    a vacation before.
  C. This is her first trip
    across the ocean.

29. A. Diana refused to talk
    about the accident.
  B. Diana promised to
    tell the woman later.
  C. Something stopped
    their conversation.

30. A. Take out the old
    carpet.
  B. Find out how big the
    floor is.
  C. Clean the floor well.

初級英語聽力檢定 ③ 詳解

第一部份

Look at the picture for question 1.

1. (**A**) Where did he put the jam?
   A. On the bread.
   B. In the toaster.
   C. With a knife.

   * put〔put〕v. 放　　jam〔dʒæm〕n. 果醬
   bread〔brɛd〕n. 麵包
   toaster〔'tostɚ〕n. 烤麵包機
   with〔wɪθ〕prep. 用　　knife〔naɪf〕n. 刀子

Look at the picture for question 2.

2. (**B**) Who won the game?
   A. They are playing chess.
   B. The man on the right.
   C. It's a king.

   * win〔wɪn〕v. 贏（三態變化為：win-won-won）
   game〔gem〕n. 比賽
   play〔ple〕v. 下（棋）
   chess〔tʃɛs〕n. 西洋棋
   right〔raɪt〕n. 右邊　　king〔kɪŋ〕n. 國王

Look at the picture for question 3.

3. (**B**) To whom will he give the bone?

    A. For dinner.

    B. The puppy.

    C. A boy.

    * whom〔hum〕*pron.* 誰（who 的受格）

      give〔gɪv〕*v.* 給　　bone〔bon〕*n.* 骨頭

      dinner〔'dɪnɚ〕*n.* 晚餐

      puppy〔'pʌpɪ〕*n.* 未滿一歲的小狗

Look at the picture for question 4.

4. (**C**) How does she feel?

    A. She cannot see.

    B. His hands.

    C. She is surprised.

    * feel〔fil〕*v.* 覺得

      see〔si〕*v.* 看見（三態變化為：see-saw-seen）

      hand〔hænd〕*n.* 手　surprised〔sə'praɪzd〕*adj.* 驚訝的

Look at the picture for question 5.

5. (**C**) What did the man give?

    A. A beggar.

    B. In the hat.

    C. A coin.

    * beggar〔'bɛgɚ〕*n.* 乞丐　　hat〔hæt〕*n.* 帽子

      coin〔kɔɪn〕*n.* 硬幣

Look at the picture for question 6.

6. (**B**) What day is it?

    A. June 15, 2005.   B. Thursday.

    C. The sixth.

  * ***What day is it?*** 今天星期幾？

    June〔dʒun〕*n.* 六月

    Thursday〔'θɝzde, -dɪ〕*n.* 星期四

    the sixth　（某月的）六日

Look at the picture for question 7.

7. (**B**) Where is the man sleeping?

    A. The boss is behind him.

    B. At his office.

    C. It fell on the floor.

  * sleep〔slip〕*v.* 睡覺　　boss〔bɔs〕*n.* 老闆

    behind〔bɪ'haɪnd〕*prep.* 在⋯後面

    office〔'ɔfɪs〕*n.* 辦公室　　fall〔fɔl〕*v.* 落下

    floor〔flor〕*n.* 地板

Look at the picture for question 8.

8. (**A**) What meal is he eating?

    A. Breakfast.   B. A happy meal.

    C. An egg.

  * meal〔mil〕*n.* 一餐

    breakfast〔'brɛkfəst〕*n.* 早餐　　egg〔ɛg〕*n.* 蛋

Look at the picture for question 9.

9. (**C**) What does she do before eating?

    A. Yes, she is eating.

    B. The woman made it.

    C. She prays.

    * before〔bɪˈfor〕prep. 在⋯之前

      make〔mek〕v. 做   pray〔pre〕v. 祈禱

Look at the picture for question 10.

10. (**A**) How does the room look?

    A. It is a mess.

    B. Yes, it's her room.

    C. She looks ashamed.

    * look〔luk〕v. 看起來   mess〔mɛs〕n. 亂七八糟；混亂

      ashamed〔əˈʃemd〕adj. 感到慚愧的

第二部份

11. (**C**) How much pie is there?

    A. It's NT$150 per slice.

    B. It's an apple pie.

    C. There is only a quarter left.

    * pie〔paɪ〕n. 派   per〔pɚ〕prep. 每⋯

      slice〔slaɪs〕n. 片   *apple pie* 蘋果派

      only〔ˈonlɪ〕adv. 只有   quarter〔ˈkwɔrtɚ〕n. 四分之一

      left〔lɛft〕adj. 剩下的

12. (**A**) Do you think Dan is chubby?

    A. No, I think he's in good shape.

    B. No, he's not married.

    C. No, you're not.

    * chubby〔'tʃʌbɪ〕adj. 圓胖的

      in good shape 身體健康；體態苗條

      married〔'mærɪd〕adj. 結婚的；已婚的

13. (**C**) How did it go at the bookstore?

    A. I took the number 86 bus.

    B. Yes. I went yesterday.

    C. I got the last copy of the *Harry Potter* book.

    * go〔go〕v.（事情）進展   bookstore〔'buk,stor〕n. 書店

      take〔tek〕v. 搭乘（交通工具）

      number〔'nʌmbɚ〕n. 第～號   get〔gɛt〕v. 買

      last〔læst〕adj. 最後的

      copy〔'kɑpɪ〕n. 一本（表同一書籍的本數單位）

      Harry Potter 哈利波特（小說名）

14. (**B**) Can you spell that?

    A. Yes, it's nice.

    B. W－I－L－L－I－A－M

    C. I got an A.

    * spell〔spɛl〕v. 拼（字）   nice〔naɪs〕adj. 好的

      William〔'wɪljəm〕n. 威廉（男子名）

      get〔gɛt〕v. 得到（成績）   A〔e〕n.（成績）甲等

15. (**B**) Where is the entrance to the building?

    A. Yes, it's open.

    B. It's on the north side.

    C. The phone number is 2189-6707.

    * entrance〔'ɛntrəns〕n. 入口
      building〔'bɪldɪŋ〕n. 建築物；大樓
      open〔'opən〕adj. 開著的
      north〔nɔrθ〕adj. 北方的　　side〔saɪd〕n. 邊
      phone〔fon〕n. 電話（= telephone）
      phone number 電話號碼

16. (**C**) Can you stay for supper?

    A. Yes, I did.

    B. Okay. I'll meet you there.

    C. I'd be delighted.

    * **stay for ~** 為~留下來　　okay〔'o'ke〕adv. 好（= OK）
      meet〔mit〕v. 和…見面（三態變化為：meet-met-met）
      there〔ðɛr〕adv. 在那裡
      delighted〔dɪ'laɪtɪd〕adj. 很高興的
      I'd be delighted. 我很樂意。

17. (**A**) Did you feel the earthquake?

    A. Yes. It was terrible.

    B. Yes, I was.

    C. No, I can't.

    * feel〔fil〕v. 感覺到　　earthquake〔'ɝθ,kwek〕n. 地震
      terrible〔'tɛləbḷ〕adj. 可怕的

18. (**A**) There is no furniture in the house.

A. The sofa will be delivered tomorrow.

B. No wonder it's so hot.

C. That's because they are away on vacation.

* furniture〔'fɜnɪtʃə〕*n.* 家具

sofa〔'sofə〕*n.* 沙發

deliver〔dɪ'lɪvə〕*v.* 遞送

wonder〔'wʌndə〕*n.* 驚奇的事

no wonder 難怪　　so〔so〕*adv.* 如此地

hot〔hɑt〕*adj.* 熱的

because〔bɪ'kɔz〕*conj.* 因為

away〔ə'we〕*adv.* 離去

vacation〔ve'keʃən〕*n.* 假期

on vacation 在休假中；在度假

19. (**B**) Did the telephone ring?

A. No, I didn't.

B. No. It was the doorbell.

C. Yes, I called you yesterday.

* telephone〔'tɛlə,fon〕*n.* 電話

ring〔rɪŋ〕*v.* (鈴) 響 (三態變化為：ring-rang-rung)

doorbell〔'dor,bɛl〕*n.* 門鈴

call〔kɔl〕*v.* 打電話給～

20. (**A**) Who caused the accident?

      A. A truck driver.

      B. It was a red light.

      C. No one was hurt.

* cause〔kɔz〕v. 造成
  accident〔'æksədənt〕n. 意外
  truck〔trʌk〕n. 卡車　　driver〔'draɪvɚ〕n. 駕駛人
  red light 紅燈　　hurt〔hɝt〕v. 傷害（三態同形）

第三部份

21. (**C**) M: What are you looking for?

      W: My purse. I left it on that chair.

      M: Well, it seems to have disappeared.

      Question: What is wrong?

      A. The chair has disappeared.

      B. The purse left.

      C. The purse is missing.

* **look for** 尋找　　purse〔pɝs〕n. 錢包
  leave〔liv〕v. 留下　　well〔wɛl〕interj. 嗯
  seem〔sim〕v. 似乎
  disappear〔,dɪsə'pɪr〕v. 消失
  What is wrong? 怎麼了？　　leave〔liv〕v. 離開
  missing〔'mɪsɪŋ〕adj. 失蹤的；找不到的

22. (**A**)　M：How about a game of Frisbee?

W：We can't play that in the house.

M：How about the yard?

W：Still too small.

Question：Why can't they play Frisbee?

A. There is not enough room.

B. The Frisbee is too small.

C. They cannot go outside.

* ***How about～?*** ～如何；～怎麼樣?

Frisbee〔'frɪzbɪ〕*n.* 飛盤　　yard〔jɑrd〕*n.* 院子

still〔stɪl〕*adv.* 仍然　　room〔rum〕*n.* 空間

outside〔'aʊt'saɪd〕*n.* 外面

23. (**A**)　M：I ordered some books online.

W：Why didn't you just go to the bookstore?

M：They're not available there.

Question：Why did the man buy books online?

A. The local bookstore does not sell them.

B. It is cheaper than buying them at the bookstore.

C. He can buy things online at any time.

* order〔'ɔrdɚ〕*v.* 訂購

online〔'ɑn,laɪn〕*adv.* 線上地；在網路上 (= *on-line*)

available〔ə'veləbḷ〕*adj.* 可獲得的

local〔'lokḷ〕*adj.* 當地的　　sell〔sɛl〕*v.* 賣

cheaper〔'tʃipɚ〕*adj.* 較便宜的 (cheap 的比較級)

things〔θɪŋz〕*n. pl.* 東西　　***at any time*** 隨時

24. (**B**) M: Where is the bird?

W: I let him out for some exercise.

M: You'd better put him back in. I'm going to open the windows.

Question: Why must the bird return to the cage?

A. It refuses to exercise.

B. It might escape through a window.

C. It might make the house dirty.

* bird 〔 bɝd 〕 *n.* 鳥　　 let 〔 lɛt 〕 *v.* 讓

exercise 〔'ɛksə͵saɪz 〕 *n.* 運動　 *v.* 運動

had better + ***V.*** 最好～　　 put 〔 pʊt 〕 *v.* 放

back 〔 bæk 〕 *adv.* 回原處　　 open 〔'opən 〕 *v.* 打開

window 〔'wɪndo 〕 *n.* 窗戶

must 〔 mʌst 〕 *aux.* 必須　　 return 〔 rɪ'tɝn 〕 *v.* 返回

cage 〔 kedʒ 〕 *n.* 籠子　　 refuse 〔 rɪ'fjuz 〕 *v.* 拒絕

might 〔 maɪt 〕 *aux.* 可能　　 escape 〔 ə'skep 〕 *v.* 逃走

through 〔 θru 〕 *prep.* 經過；通過

make 〔 mek 〕 *v.* 使　　 dirty 〔'dɝtɪ 〕 *adj.* 髒的

25. (**B**) M: Are you going to the cafeteria?

W: No. I already had lunch.

M: That was early!

W: Yes. I wanted to beat the crowd.

Question: Why did the woman eat lunch early?

A. She wants to exercise after lunch.

B. The cafeteria is full of people at lunchtime.

C. Eating lunch early is fashionable.

* cafeteria〔ˌkæfəˈtɪrɪə〕 n. 自助餐廳

　already〔ɔlˈrɛdɪ〕adv. 已經　　have〔hæv〕v. 吃

　lunch〔lʌntʃ〕n. 午餐　　early〔ˈɝlɪ〕adj. 早的　adv. 早

　beat〔bit〕v. 比…先到　　crowd〔kraud〕n. 人群

　after〔ˈæftɚ〕prep. 在…之後　　**be full of**… 充滿了…

　people〔ˈpipḷ〕n. pl. 人

　lunchtime〔ˈlʌntʃˌtaɪm〕n. 午餐時間

　fashionable〔ˈfæʃənəbḷ〕adj. 流行的；時髦的

26. (**A**)　M：Do you take a nap at school?

　　　W：No, I usually study during the break.

　　　M：I have to sleep. Otherwise, I'll sleep in class.

　　Question：Does the man sleep at school?

　　A. Yes, he sleeps during the break time.

　　B. Yes, he often sleeps during class.

　　C. No, he usually studies instead.

* nap〔næp〕n. 午睡　　**take a nap** 睡午覺

　usually〔ˈjuʒʊəlɪ〕adv. 通常　　study〔ˈstʌdɪ〕v. 研讀

　during〔ˈdjʊrɪŋ〕prep. 在…期間

　break〔brek〕n. 休息時間　　**have to** 必須

　sleep〔slip〕v. 睡覺

　otherwise〔ˈʌðɚˌwaɪz〕adv. 否則

　in class 上課中　　instead〔ɪnˈstɛd〕adv. 作為代替

27. (**C**)　M：The freezer is broken.

W：Uh-oh.　What should we do?

M：I think we should eat the ice cream right away.

Question：Why does the man want to eat?

A.　He needs energy to fix the freezer.

B.　He has a cold.

C.　He is afraid the food will melt.

* freezer〔'frizɚ〕n. 冰箱

　broken〔'brokən〕adj. 壞了的

　uh-oh〔'ʌ'o〕interj. 唔哦（遭遇問題時的感嘆語）

　should〔ʃud〕aux. 應該　　***ice cream*** 冰淇淋

　right away 馬上　　energy〔'ɛnədʒɪ〕n. 精力；活力

　fix〔fɪks〕v. 修理　　cold〔kold〕n. 感冒

　have a cold 感冒

　afraid〔ə'fred〕adj. 害怕的；擔心的

　melt〔mɛlt〕v. 融化

28. (**C**)　M：Have you been overseas before?

W：No.　This is my first trip.

M：How exciting for you.

W：Yes, but I'm a little bit nervous too.

Question：Why is the woman nervous?

A.　She has never been on a ship before.

B.　She has never taken a vacation before.

C.　This is her first trip across the ocean.

* overseas〔'ovə'siz〕*adv.* 到海外
before〔bɪ'for〕*adv.* 以前　　first〔fɝst〕*adj.* 第一的
trip〔trɪp〕*n.* 旅行　　exciting〔ɪk'saɪtɪŋ〕*adj.* 令人興奮的
How exciting for you. 你一定很興奮。
bit〔bɪt〕*n.* 一點；少許　　***a little bit*** 一點點
nervous〔'nɝvəs〕*adj.* 緊張的　　never〔'nɛvə〕*adv.* 從未
have never been 從未　　ship〔ʃɪp〕*n.* 船
take a vacation 度假　　across〔ə'krɔs〕*prep.* 橫越過
ocean〔'oʃən〕*n.* 海洋

29. (**C**)　M：Did you talk to Diana about the accident?

W：I tried to but we were interrupted.

M：Well, try again later. I'd like to know what happened.

Question：What happened during the woman's
conversation with Diana?

A. Diana refused to talk about the accident.

B. Diana promised to tell the woman later.

C. Something stopped their conversation.

* ***talk to*** sb. ***about*** sth.　和某人談論某事
accident〔'æksədənt〕*n.* 意外　　try〔traɪ〕*v.* 試著
interrupt〔ˌɪntə'rʌpt〕*v.* 打斷（談話）
well〔wɛl〕*interj.* 好吧（表讓步）
again〔ə'gɛn〕*adv.* 再一次　　later〔'letə〕*adv.* 稍後
would like to V. 想要～（= *want to V.*）
happen〔'hæpən〕*v.* 發生
conversation〔ˌkɑnvə'seʃən〕*n.* 對話
refuse〔rɪ'fjuz〕*v.* 拒絕
promise〔'prɑmɪs〕*v.* 保證；答應　　tell〔tɛl〕*v.* 告訴
something〔'sʌmθɪŋ〕*pron.* 某事　　stop〔stɑp〕*v.* 使…停止

30. (**B**) M：I'd like to get a new carpet.

W：So would I.

M：Then let's measure the floor.

Question：What are they going to do?

A. Take out the old carpet.

B. Find out how big the floor is.

C. Clean the floor well.

* get〔gɛt〕v. 買　　carpet〔'kɑrpɪt〕n. 地毯

So would I. 我也是。（在此表「我也想要。」）

measure〔'mɛʒɚ〕v. 測量　　floor〔flor〕n. 地板

take out 除去…；把…拿出去　　old〔old〕adj. 老舊的

find out 查出；找出　　*how big* 多大

clean〔klin〕v. 打掃　　well〔wɛl〕adv. 充分地；好好地

全民英語能力分級檢定測驗

初級測驗④

一、聽力測驗

本測驗分三部份，全爲三選一之選擇題，每部份各 10 題，共 30 題，作答時間約 20 分鐘。

第一部份：看圖辨義

本部份共 10 題，試題冊上每題有一個圖片，請聽錄音機播出一個相關的問題，與 A、B、C 三個英語敘述後，選一個與所看到圖片最相符的答案，並在答案紙上相對的圓圈內塗黑作答。每題播出一遍，問題及選項均不印在試題冊上。

例：（看）

NT\$80　　NT\$50

（聽）

Look at the picture.　How much is the hamburger?

A.　It's eighty dollars.

B.　It's fifty-five dollars.

C.　It's eighteen dollars.

正確答案爲 A

Question 1

Question 2

Question 3

Question 4

請翻頁

Question 5

Question 6

Question 7

Question 8

Question 9

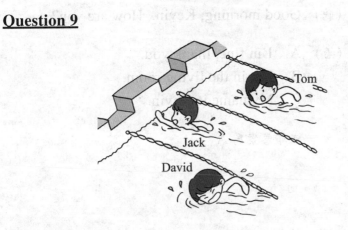

Question 10

請翻頁 ⃗

第二部份： 問答

本部份共 10 題，每題錄音機會播出一個問句或直述句，
每題播出一次，聽後請從試題冊上 A、B、C 三個選項
中，選出一個最適合的回答或回應，並在答案紙上塗黑
作答。

例：

（聽） Good morning, Kevin. How are you?

（看） A.　I'm fine, thank you.
　　　 B.　I'm in the living room.
　　　 C.　My name is Kevin.

正確答案為 A

11. A. I will be here.
　　B. Yes, Jack was here.
　　C. No, I wasn't.

12. A. It really hurts.
　　B. It's my right hand.
　　C. I cut it.

13. A. Yes, let's call him now.

B. I think we should call him Spot.

C. No, I don't think we called him.

14. A. It was just one week.

B. Just last night.

C. I brought back a gift for you.

15. A. Here you are.

B. How can I help you?

C. I will read it soon.

16. A. No, I went last year.

B. Yes, I was.

C. Yes, I did.

17. A. It's a book.

B. It's my sister's birthday today.

C. Oh, thank you!

18. A. It's about two hours from here.

B. For two days.

C. Yes, I will be there a long time.

19. A. Yes, she did.

B. Of course, you can, Mary.

C. Here it is.

20. A. Yes, I do.

B. Thank you.

C. It's over there.

請 翻 頁 ⟹

第三部份： 簡短對話

本部份共 10 題，每題錄音機會播出一段對話及一個相關
的問題，每題播出兩次，聽後請從試題冊上 A、B、C 三
個選項中，選出一個最適合的回答，並在答案紙上塗黑
作答。

例：

（聽）(Woman) Good afternoon, ...Mr. Davis?

(Man) Yes. I have an appointment with Dr. Sanders at two o'clock. My son Tommy has a fever.

(Woman) Oh, that's too bad. Well, please have a seat, Mr. Davis. Dr. Sanders will be right with you.

Question: Where did this conversation take place?

（看）A. In a post office.

B. In a restaurant.

C. In a doctor's office.

正確答案爲 C

21. A. New friends and
neighbors.
B. Clerk and customer.
C. Regular
correspondents.

22. A. She doesn't like it.
B. It is the least
expensive.
C. She agrees with the
man.

23. A. They are standing on
it.
B. On the main gate.
C. On a map of the park.

24. A. He is a waiter.
B. He is the woman's
husband.
C. He is one of twelve
guests.

25. A. They are too
expensive.
B. They are sent to
other countries.
C. The bananas are
not of good quality.

請 翻 頁 ||⇒

26. A. She does not spend her free time studying.
　　B. She makes too many jokes in class.
　　C. She did not pay enough for the class.

27. A. The factory makes 5000 earrings a week.
　　B. 5000 people work at the factory.
　　C. The workers can earn 5000 per week.

28. A. Some birds.
　　B. Their neighbors.
　　C. Their guests.

29. A. She doesn't really need a radio.
　　B. The salesperson didn't tell her it was different.
　　C. It sounded the same as the expensive one.

30. A. No, because he does not practice often enough.
　　B. Yes, because he started playing when he was a child.
　　C. No, because he did not start playing when he was a child.

初級英語聽力檢定④詳解

第一部份

Look at the picture for question 1.

1. (**B**) What will he do next?

    A. He has some glue.

    B. He will mail the letter.

    C. He is writing a letter.

* next〔nɛkst〕*adv.* 接著；接下來

  glue〔glu〕*n.* 膠水　　mail〔mel〕*v.* 郵寄

  letter〔'lɛtɚ〕*n.* 信　　write〔raɪt〕*v.* 寫

Look at the picture for question 2.

2. (**C**) Where is he playing the game?

    A. Because it is fun.

    B. He likes it very much.

    C. On his computer.

* play〔ple〕*v.* 玩　　game〔gem〕*n.* 遊戲

  because〔bɪ'kɔz〕*conj.* 因為

  fun〔fʌn〕*adj.* 好玩的；有趣的

  like〔laɪk〕*v.* 喜歡

  very much 很；非常（修飾動詞，表程度）

  computer〔kəm'pjutɚ〕*n.* 電腦

Look at the picture for question 3.

3. (**B**) Who is the man in front of the counter?

    A. He is a clerk.   B. He is a customer.

    C. He is a cook.

    * *in front of* ~ 在～前面   counter 〔'kaʊntɚ 〕 *n.* 櫃台

    clerk 〔 klɜk 〕 *n.* 店員   customer 〔'kʌstəmɚ 〕 *n.* 顧客

    cook 〔 kʊk 〕 *n.* 廚師

Look at the picture for question 4.

4. (**B**) Why doesn't he like the fruit?

    A. No, he doesn't like it.

    B. It smells bad.

    C. It is too expensive.

    * fruit 〔 frut 〕 *n.* 水果   smell 〔 smɛl 〕 *v.* 聞起來；有…氣味

    bad 〔 bæd 〕 *adj.* 不好的

    expensive 〔 ɪk'spɛnsɪv 〕 *adj.* 昂貴的

Look at the picture for question 5.

5. (**A**) What is the reporter doing?

    A. He is asking questions.

    B. He has a microphone.

    C. He is friendly.

    * reporter 〔 rɪ'portɚ 〕 *n.* 記者   ask 〔 æsk 〕 *v.* 問

    question 〔'kwɛstʃən 〕 *n.* 問題

    microphone 〔'maɪkrə,fon 〕 *n.* 麥克風

    friendly 〔'frɛndlɪ 〕 *adj.* 友善的

Look at the picture for question 6.

6. (**A**) How does the girl go to school?

　A. She rides a bike.

　B. Yes, she is going to school.

　C. Because it is too far to walk.

　* ride〔raɪd〕v. 騎　　bike〔baɪk〕n. 腳踏車
　　because〔bɪ'kɔz〕conj. 因為
　　too…to～　太…以致不能～　　far〔fɑr〕adj. 遠的
　　walk〔wɔk〕v. 走路

Look at the picture for question 7.

7. (**C**) What are they doing in the boat?

　A. It is a dragon boat.

　B. They cannot swim.

　C. They are racing.

　* boat〔bot〕n. 船　　dragon〔'drægən〕n. 龍
　　dragon boat 龍舟　　swim〔swɪm〕v. 游泳
　　race〔res〕v. 競賽

Look at the picture for question 8.

8. (**C**) What is on the sign?

　A. One way.

　B. On the street.

　C. An arrow.

　* sign〔saɪn〕n. 標誌　　**one way** 單行道
　　street〔strit〕n. 街道　　arrow〔'æro〕n. 箭頭

Look at the picture for question 9.

9. (**A**) Who is in second place?

    A. Tom.

    B. Jack.

    C. David.

    * second〔'sɛkənd〕adj. 第二的

    second place 第二名

Look at the picture for question 10.

10. (**B**) What are they waiting for?

    A. A long line.

    B. Tickets.

    C. They have been waiting a long time.

    * ***wait for*** 等待   long〔lɔŋ〕adj. 長的

    line〔laɪn〕n. 隊伍   ticket〔'tɪkɪt〕n. 票

    time〔taɪm〕n. 時間

    They have been waiting a long time. 他們等了很久了。

第二部份

11. (**C**) Were you here yesterday?

    A. I will be here.

    B. Yes, Jack was here.

    C. No, I wasn't.

    * here〔hɪr〕adv. 在（到）這裡

    yesterday〔'jɛstəde, -dɪ〕adv. 昨天

12. (**C**) How did you hurt your hand?

  A. It really hurts.

  B. It's my right hand.

  C. I cut it.

  * hurt〔hɝt〕*v.* 使受傷；疼痛

  really〔'riəlɪ〕*adv.* 眞地 right〔raɪt〕*adj.* 右邊的

  hand〔hænd〕*n.* 手 cut〔kʌt〕*v.* 切；割傷

13. (**A**) Don't you think we should call him?

  A. Yes, let's call him now.

  B. I think we should call him Spot.

  C. No, I don't think we called him.

  * think〔θɪŋk〕*v.* 認爲（三態變化爲：think-thought-thought）

  should〔ʃud〕*aux.* 應該

  call〔kɔl〕*v.* 打電話給～；稱呼

  spot〔spɑt〕*n.* 斑點（美國人常將有斑點的狗取名爲 Spot）

14. (**B**) When did you get back from your vacation?

  A. It was just one week.

  B. Just last night.

  C. I brought back a gift for you.

  * ***get back from***⋯ 從⋯回來

  vacation〔ve'keʃən〕*n.* 假期

  just〔dʒʌst〕*adv.* 只是；才

  week〔wik〕*n.* 星期 ***last night*** 昨晚

  bring〔brɪŋ〕*v.* 帶來（三態變化爲：bring-brought-brought）

  bring back 帶回 gift〔gɪft〕*n.* 禮物

15. (**A**) Do me a favor and hand me that book, will you?

    A. Here you are.

    B. How can I help you?

    C. I will read it soon.

    * favor〔'fevɚ〕*n.* 恩惠;幫助

    do me a favor 幫我一個忙

    hand〔hænd〕*v.* 拿給

    Here you are. 你要的東西在這裡;拿去吧。(= *Here it is.*)

    help〔hɛlp〕*v.* 幫助

    How can I help you? 我能怎麼幫你?

    read〔rid〕*v.* 讀   soon〔sun〕*adv.* 馬上;很快地

16. (**C**) Did you say that you've been to Japan?

    A. No, I went last year.

    B. Yes, I was.

    C. Yes, I did.

    * ***have been to*** ~ 曾經去過~

    Japan〔dʒə'pæn〕*n.* 日本   ***last year*** 去年

17. (**B**) Who's the present for?

    A. It's a book.

    B. It's my sister's birthday today.

    C. Oh, thank you!

    * present〔'prɛzn̩t〕*n.* 禮物

    birthday〔'bɝθ,de〕*n.* 生日

    oh〔o〕*interj.* 喔(因驚訝所發出的感嘆)

18. (**B**) How long will you be in Keelung?

    A. It's about two hours from here.

    B. For two days.

    C. Yes, I will be there a long time.

    * ***How long ~?*** ~多久？

    Keelung〔'ki'lʌŋ〕*n.* 基隆

    How long will you be in Keelung? 你將在基隆待多久？

    about〔ə'baʊt〕*adv.* 大約   hour〔aʊr〕*n.* 小時

    for〔fɔr〕*prep.* 持續

19. (**A**) Did Mary ask you for a ride?

    A. Yes, she did.

    B. Of course, you can, Mary.

    C. Here it is.

    * ***ask for*** 請求   ride〔raɪd〕*n.* 搭便車

    of course 當然

    Here it is. 你要的東西在這裡；拿去吧

20. (**B**) I have that book you wanted.

    A. Yes, I do.

    B. Thank you.

    C. It's over there.

    * want〔wɑnt〕*v.* 想要   ***over there*** 在那裡

第三部份

21. (**B**) M：Do you know that woman?

W：Not personally, but she is a regular customer.

M：What's her name?

W：I'm sorry, but I don't know.

Question：What is the relationship between the two women?

A. New friends and neighbors.

B. Clerk and customer.

C. Regular correspondents.

* personally〔'pɝsn̩lɪ〕*adv.* 私下地；我個人
  regular〔'rɛgjələ〕*adj.* 定期的；固定的
  customer〔'kʌstəmə〕*n.* 顧客
  regular customer 老主顧
  relationship〔rɪ'leʃən‚ʃɪp〕*n.* 關係
  between〔bə'twin〕*prep.* 在…之間
  neighbor〔'nebə〕*n.* 鄰居　　clerk〔klɝk〕*n.* 店員
  correspondent〔‚kɔrə'spandənt〕*n.* 通信的人

22. (**A**) M：What do you think of the apartments we've seen so far?

W：The one on Baker Street has a lot of light and is quiet.

M：True. I like the one on Monroe Street, though.

W：I think that one has the least to offer.

Question：What does the woman think of the Monroe Street apartment?

A. She doesn't like it.

B. It is the least expensive.

C. She agrees with the man.

* **think of** 認為　　apartment〔ə'pɑrtmənt〕n. 公寓

　see〔si〕v. 看（三態變化為：see-saw-seen）

　so far 到目前為止　　light〔laɪt〕n. 光線

　quiet〔'kwaɪət〕adj. 安靜的　　true〔tru〕adj. 沒錯；真的

　though〔ðo〕adv. 可是；不過

　least〔list〕pron. 最少　adv. 最少；最不（little 的最高級）

　offer〔'ɔfɚ〕v. 提供　　**agree with …** 與…意見一致

23. (**C**)　M：I don't understand this map.

　　　W：This green area is the whole park, and this star
　　　　　indicates where we are now.

　　　M：At the main gate?

　　　W：Right.

　　　Question：Where is the star?

　A. They are standing on it.

　B. On the main gate.

　C. On a map of the park.

* understand〔ˌʌndɚ'stænd〕v. 了解；懂

　map〔mæp〕n. 地圖　　green〔grin〕adj. 綠色的

　area〔'ɛrɪə〕n. 地區；區域　　whole〔hol〕adj. 整個的

　park〔pɑrk〕n. 公園　　star〔stɑr〕n. 星星

　indicate〔'ɪndəˌket〕v. 指出；表示

　main〔men〕adj. 主要的　　gate〔get〕n. 大門

　right〔raɪt〕adv. 正確地；對地　　stand〔stænd〕v. 站

24. (**C**) M: How many guests are you expecting tonight?

W: Twelve, including you.

M: Can I do anything to help?

W: No.　Just relax until the others get here.

Question: Who is the man?

A. He is a waiter.

B. He is the woman's husband.

C. He is one of twelve guests.

* guest〔gɛst〕*n.* 客人　　expect〔ɪk'spɛkt〕*v.* 期待

tonight〔tə'naɪt〕*adv.* 今晚

including〔ɪn'kludɪŋ〕*prep.* 包括

anything〔'ɛnɪ,θɪŋ〕*pron.* 任何事

help〔hɛlp〕*v.* 幫忙

just〔dʒʌst〕*adv.* 就…（委婉的祈使語氣）

relax〔rɪ'læks〕*v.* 放輕鬆　　until〔ən'tɪl〕*conj.* 直到

other〔'ʌðɚ〕*pron.* 其他的人

the others 其他的人（不包括在場的人）

get〔gɛt〕*v.* 抵達　　waiter〔'wetɚ〕*n.* 服務生

husband〔'hʌzbənd〕*n.* 丈夫

25. (**B**) M: We grow so many bananas here.　How come I can never find any in the market?

W: Most of them are exported now.

Question: Why is it difficult to find bananas in the market?

A. They are too expensive.

B. They are sent to other countries.

C. The bananas are not of good quality.

* grow〔gro〕v. 種植　　banana〔bə'nænə〕n. 香蕉
How come~? 怎麼會～；為什麼～？
never〔'nɛvɚ〕adv. 從未　　find〔faɪnd〕v. 發現
any〔'ɛnɪ〕pron. 任何人或物　　market〔'markɪt〕n. 市場
most of~ 大部分的～　　export〔ɪks'port〕v. 出口
difficult〔'dɪfə,kʌlt〕adj. 困難的
send〔sɛnd〕v. 寄；送　　country〔'kʌntrɪ〕n. 國家
quality〔'kwɑlətɪ〕n. 品質　　***of good quality*** 品質好的

26. (**A**) M：Becky's grades are terrible.

W：It's because she spends all her free time on comics.

M：She needs to start studying and pay attention in class.

Question：Why is Becky doing poorly in school?

A. She does not spend her free time studying.

B. She makes too many jokes in class.

C. She did not pay enough for the class.

* grade〔gred〕n. 成績　　terrible〔'tɛrəbl̩〕adj. 很糟的
because〔bɪ'kɔz〕conj. 因為
spend〔spɛnd〕v. 花（時間）
free〔fri〕adj. 空閒的　　comics〔'kɑmɪks〕n. pl. 漫畫書
need〔nid〕v. 需要　　start〔start〕v. 開始
study〔'stʌdɪ〕v. 讀書　　pay〔pe〕v. 給予（注意）；付錢
attention〔ə'tɛnʃən〕n. 注意；專心　　***pay attention*** 專心
in class 上課期間　　do〔du〕v. （課業）表現
poorly〔'pʊrlɪ〕adv. 差勁地　　joke〔dʒok〕n. 笑話
make a joke 說笑話　　enough〔ə'nʌf〕adv. 足夠地

27. (**B**) M：This is a large factory.

W：It employs 5000 people.

M：And do they make much?

W：They earn enough.

Question：Which of the following is true?

A. The factory makes 5000 earrings a week.

B. 5000 people work at the factory.

C. The workers can earn 5000 per week.

* large〔 lɑrdʒ 〕*adj.* 大的　　factory〔'fæktrɪ 〕*n.* 工廠
employ〔 ɪm'plɔɪ 〕*v.* 雇用
make〔 mek 〕*v.* 賺（錢）；製造
much〔 mʌtʃ 〕*pron.* 大量；很多（當單數用）
earn〔 ɝn 〕*v.* 賺（錢）　　which〔 hwɪtʃ 〕*pron.* 哪一個
following〔'fɑləwɪŋ 〕*adj.* 下列的
the following 下列的物（人）　　true〔 tru 〕*adj.* 正確的
earrings〔'ɪr͵rɪŋz 〕*n. pl.* 耳環
week〔 wik 〕*n.* 星期　　work〔 wɝk 〕*v.* 工作
worker〔'wɝkɚ 〕*n.* 工人　　per〔 pɚ 〕*prep.* 每一…

28. (**A**) M：Who made this mess on the balcony?

W：The pigeons must have done it.

M：I wish they would move somewhere else!

Question：Who made the mess?

A. Some birds.

B. Their neighbors.

C. Their guests.

* make〔mek〕v. 製造　　mess〔mɛs〕n. 亂七八糟；混亂
balcony〔'bælkənɪ〕n. 陽台　　pigeon〔'pɪdʒɪn〕n. 鴿子
must〔mʌst〕aux. 一定　　done〔dʌn〕v. do 的過去分詞
wish〔wɪʃ〕v. 希望　　move〔muv〕v. 遷移；搬家
somewhere〔'sʌm,whɛr〕adv. 某處
else〔ɛls〕adv. 其他　　bird〔bɝd〕n. 鳥
neighbor〔'nebɚ〕n. 鄰居　　guest〔gɛst〕n. 客人

29. (**C**) M：Why did you buy the cheaper radio?

W：I couldn't hear any difference between them.

M：Well, I guess there's no sense spending money on
something you don't need.

Question：Why did the woman buy a cheap radio?

A. She doesn't really need a radio.

B. The salesperson didn't tell her it was different.

C. It sounded the same as the expensive one.

* cheaper〔'tʃipɚ〕adj. 較便宜的（cheap 的比較級）
radio〔'redɪ,o〕n. 收音機　　hear〔hɪr〕v. 聽到；聽見
difference〔'dɪfərəns〕n. 不同
between〔bə'twin〕prep. 在…之間
well〔wɛl〕interj. 嗯；好吧（表讓步）
guess〔gɛs〕v. 猜想；認為　　sense〔sɛns〕n. 意義；道理
spend〔spɛnd〕v. 花（錢）
something〔'sʌmθɪŋ〕pron. 某物
buy〔baɪ〕v. 買（三態變化為：buy-bought-bought）
really〔'rɪəlɪ〕adv. 真地
salesperson〔'selz,pɝsṇ〕n. 售貨員；店員
different〔'dɪfərənt〕adj. 不同的
sound〔saʊnd〕v. 聽起來　　***the same as*** ~ 與~相同
one〔wʌn〕pron. 一個（代替前面已提及的可數名詞 radio）

30. (**A**) M: Sue plays the piano so well.

W: That's because she started playing when she was a child.

M: So did I.

W: Yes, but Sue practices every day.

Question: Can the man play the piano well?

A. No, because he does not practice often enough.

B. Yes, because he started playing when he was a child.

C. No, because he did not start playing when he was a child.

* play〔ple〕v. 彈；演奏　　piano〔pɪ'æno〕n. 鋼琴

so〔so〕adv. 如此地　　well〔wɛl〕adv. 良好地

because〔bɪ'kɔz〕conj. 因為

start〔stɑrt〕v. 開始　　child〔tʃaɪld〕n. 小孩

So did I. 我也是。　　practice〔'præktɪs〕v. 練習

every day 每天　　often〔'ɔfən〕adv. 經常

enough〔ə'nʌf〕adv. 足夠地

全民英語能力分級檢定測驗

初級測驗⑤

　　本測驗分三部份，全為三選一之選擇題，每部份各 10 題，共 30 題，作答時間約 20 分鐘。

第一部份： 看圖辨義
　　　　　本部份共 10 題，試題冊上每題有一個圖片，請聽錄音機播出一個相關的問題，與 A、B、C 三個英語敘述後，選一個與所看到圖片最相符的答案，並在答案紙上相對的圓圈內塗黑作答。每題播出一遍，問題及選項均不印在試題冊上。

例：（看）

NT$80　　NT$50

（聽）

Look at the picture.　How much is the hamburger?

　　A.　It's eighty dollars.
　　B.　It's fifty-five dollars.
　　C.　It's eighteen dollars.

正確答案為 A

A. **Question 1**

B. **Question 2**

C. Question 3

D. Questions 4-5

請翻頁 ⟹

E. **Question 6**

F. **Question 7**

G. **Question 8**

H. Question 9

I. Question 10

請翻頁 ⫸

第二部份： 問答

本部份共10題，每題錄音機會播出一個問句或直述句，每題播出一次，聽後請從試題冊上A、B、C三個選項中，選出一個最適合的回答或回應，並在答案紙上塗黑作答。

例：

（聽） Good morning, Kevin. How are you?

（看） A. I'm fine, thank you.
　　　 B. I'm in the living room.
　　　 C. My name is Kevin.

　　　 正確答案爲 A

11. A. No. She is a housewife.
　　B. Yes. She is a firefighter.
　　C. No. She wasn't elected.

12. A. They just couldn't get along.
　　B. It went bankrupt.
　　C. It lasted ten years.

13. A. No, I can't play.
　　B. I prefer hip-hop.
　　C. George plays the piano.

14. A. Yes, but don't feed them.
　　B. They're on the playground.
　　C. No, but you can use my phone.

15. A. Tomorrow is Jim's birthday and I wanted to surprise him.
    B. I mixed all the ingredients and then put it in the oven.
    C. No, it wasn't that difficult.

16. A. He is awfully cute, isn't he?
    B. I'll try to be more quiet.
    C. Maybe we should get a fence.

17. A. That sounds great.
    B. No, I always eat breakfast.
    C. You don't need to lose weight.

18. A. Yes. I always finish my homework.
    B. Yes, I'm an optimistic person.
    C. No. I work out only twice a week.

19. A. Until 7:00.
    B. At 9 a.m., Tuesday through Sunday.
    C. Yes, it is.

20. A. No. I was on the balcony.
    B. Yes, I didn't. Sorry.
    C. No, I won't be here tomorrow.

請 翻 頁 ⫸

第三部份： 簡短對話

本部份共 10 題，每題錄音機會播出一段對話及一個相關的問題，每題播出兩次，聽後請從試題冊上 A、B、C 三個選項中，選出一個最適合的回答，並在答案紙上塗黑作答。

例：

（聽）(Woman) Good afternoon, ...Mr. Davis?

(Man) Yes. I have an appointment with Dr. Sanders at two o'clock. My son Tommy has a fever.

(Woman) Oh, that's too bad. Well, please have a seat, Mr. Davis. Dr. Sanders will be right with you.

Question: Where did this conversation take place?

（看）A. In a post office.

B. In a restaurant.

C. In a doctor's office.

正確答案為 C

21. A. She is taking a lot of subjects.
    B. They are supplied by the school.
    C. They are too expensive to leave behind.

22. A. She is strict.
    B. She is worried.
    C. She doesn't like to answer questions.

23. A. Whether or not he will go mountain climbing.
    B. That the woman is afraid to ask Anna.
    C. That Anna is afraid of high places.

24. A. It is the biggest city in the world.
    B. Beijing has a large population.
    C. Beijing is a very polluted city.

25. A. She would not have gotten sunburned.
    B. She would have played better.
    C. She wouldn't be black.

請 翻 頁 ▯⟹

26. A. He will buy 2 grams
       of medicine.
    B. He will buy the pills.
    C. He will buy the
       liquid medicine.

27. A. Every hour on the
       hour.
    B. At seven in the
       morning.
    C. In the evening.

28. A. Change his seat to
       another chair.
    B. Turn his chair
       around.
    C. Raise his chair.

29. A. His wife spends too
       much time at the
       beauty salon.
    B. His wife spends too
       much money on
       clothes.
    C. His wife had promised
       to go to the hairdresser
       last week.

30. A. She did not
       accomplish her goal.
    B. She would like to
       climb more hills.
    C. She did not climb
       very high.

初級英語聽力檢定⑤詳解

第一部份

For question number 1, please look at picture A.

1. (**A**) Who did the woman call?

    A. The police.

    B. A fight.

    C. The killer.

    * call〔kɔl〕v. 打電話給~   police〔pə'lis〕n. 警方
    fight〔faɪt〕n. 打架   killer〔'kɪlɚ〕n. 殺人者

For question number 2, please look at picture B.

2. (**C**) What is the man holding?

    A. A box.

    B. The woman.

    C. The door.

    * hold〔hold〕v. 抓住；支撐
    door〔dor〕n. 門

For question number 3, please look at picture C.

3. (**C**) Where is the man going?

    A. Take off his shoes.

    B. For a walk.

    C. Inside.

    * ***take off*** 脫掉 (↔ *put on*)   shoes〔ʃuz〕n. pl. 鞋子
    walk〔wɔk〕n. 散步   inside〔'ɪn'saɪd〕adv. 向室內

For questions number 4 and 5, please look at picture D.

4. (**B**) Where can you find a bus stop?

    A. Inside McDonald's.

    B. Across from the convenience store.

    C. At the bus station.

    * find〔faɪnd〕*v.* 找到　　***bus stop*** 公車站

    inside〔ɪn'saɪd〕*prep.* 在…裡面

    McDonald's〔mək'danḷdz〕*n.* 麥當勞

    across from … 在…的對面

    convenience〔kən'vinjəns〕*n.* 便利

    convenience store 便利商店

    bus station 公車總站

5. (**A**) Please look at picture D again.　Where is the stationery store?

    A. It is near the train station.

    B. It is opposite the temple.

    C. It is next to the police station.

    * stationery〔'steʃən,ɛrɪ〕*n.* 文具

    store〔stor〕*n.* 商店

    stationery store 文具行

    near〔nɪr〕*prep.* 在…附近

    train station 火車站

    opposite〔'apəzɪt〕*prep.* 在…對面

    temple〔'tempḷ〕*n.* 寺廟　　***next to*** ~ 在~旁邊

    police〔pə'lis〕*n.* 警察　　***police station*** 警察局

For question number 6, please look at picture E.

6. (**B**) Why are the people running?

    A. They are shaking.

    B. There is an earthquake.

    C. It is a race.

    * run〔rʌn〕*v.* 跑　　shake〔ʃek〕*v.* 發抖

    earthquake〔'ɝθ͵kwek〕*n.* 地震

    race〔res〕*n.* 賽跑

For question number 7, please look at picture F.

7. (**B**) How does the boss feel?

    A. He is increasing.

    B. He is pleased.

    C. He is sitting down.

    * boss〔bɔs〕*n.* 老闆　　feel〔fil〕*v.* 覺得

    increase〔ɪn'kris〕*v.* 增加

    pleased〔plizd〕*adj.* 高興的

    sit down 坐下

For question number 8, please look at picture G.

8. (**C**) Who has a watch?

    A. Yes, he does.

    B. No, it's a clock.

    C. The man.

    * watch〔wɑtʃ〕*n.* 錶　　clock〔klɑk〕*n.* 時鐘

For question number 9, please look at picture H.

9. (**A**) Why are people angry?

    A. It is too noisy.

    B. Yes, they are.

    C. It's not a library.

    * angry〔'æŋgrɪ〕*adj.* 生氣的   noisy〔'nɔɪzɪ〕*adj.* 吵鬧的
      library〔'laɪˌbrɛrɪ〕*n.* 圖書館

For question number 10, please look at picture I.

10. (**A**) What is the snake doing?

    A. He is swallowing an egg.

    B. He has laid an egg.

    C. He ate it.

    * snake〔snek〕*n.* 蛇   swallow〔'swɑlo〕*v.* 吞下
      egg〔ɛg〕*n.* 蛋
      lay〔le〕*v.* 下（蛋）（三態變化為：lay-laid-laid）
      eat〔it〕*v.* 吃（三態變化為：eat-ate-eaten）

第二部份

11. (**A**) Does your mother work in an office?

    A. No. She is a housewife.

    B. Yes. She is a firefighter.

    C. No. She wasn't elected.

    * work〔wɝk〕*v.* 工作   office〔'ɔfɪs〕*n.* 辦公室
      housewife〔'haʊsˌwaɪf〕*n.* 家庭主婦
      firefighter〔'faɪrˌfaɪtɚ〕*n.* 消防隊員
      elect〔ɪ'lɛkt〕*v.* （以投票）選出

12. (**A**) Why did his marriage end?

  A. They just couldn't get along.

  B. It went bankrupt.

  C. It lasted ten years.

  * marriage〔'mærɪdʒ〕*n.* 婚姻 end〔ɛnd〕*v.* 結束

  just〔dʒʌst〕*adv.* 眞地；的確

  could〔kʊd〕*aux.* can 的過去式

  get along 處得好；相處

  bankrupt〔'bæŋkrʌpt〕*adj.* 破產的 ***go bankrupt*** 破產

  last〔læst〕*v.* 持續

13. (**C**) Do you know any musicians?

  A. No, I can't play. B. I prefer hip-hop.

  C. George plays the piano.

  * musician〔mju'zɪʃən〕*n.* 音樂家 play〔ple〕*v.* 演奏

  prefer〔prɪ'fɝ〕*v.* 比較喜歡

  hip-hop〔'hɪp,hɑp〕*n.* 嘻哈（一種源自美國的流行音樂）

  George〔dʒɔrdʒ〕*n.* 喬治（男子名）

  piano〔pɪ'æno〕*n.* 鋼琴

14. (**B**) Are there any swings in the park?

  A. Yes, but don't feed them.

  B. They're on the playground.

  C. No, but you can use my phone.

  * swing〔swɪŋ〕*n.* 鞦韆 park〔pɑrk〕*n.* 公園

  feed〔fid〕*v.* 餵食

  playground〔'ple,graʊnd〕*n.* 遊樂場；操場

  use〔juz〕*v.* 使用 phone〔fon〕*n.* 電話（ = *telephone* ）

15. (**B**) How did you make this cake?

 A. Tomorrow is Jim's birthday and I wanted to surprise him.

 B. I mixed all the ingredients and then put it in the oven.

 C. No, it wasn't that difficult.

 * make〔mek〕v. 做　　cake〔kek〕n. 蛋糕
 tomorrow〔tə'maro〕n. 明天　　want〔wɑnt〕v. 想要
 surprise〔sə'praɪz〕v. 使驚訝
 mix〔mɪks〕v. 混合；攪拌
 ingredient〔ɪn'gridɪənt〕n. (烹飪) 原料
 put〔put〕v. 放　　oven〔'ʌvən〕n. 烤箱
 that〔ðæt〕adv. 那樣地；那麼
 difficult〔'dɪfə,kʌlt〕adj. 困難的

16. (**C**) The neighbors are complaining about our dog again.

 A. He is awfully cute, isn't he?

 B. I'll try to be more quiet.

 C. Maybe we should get a fence.

 * neighbor〔'nebɚ〕n. 鄰居
 complain〔kəm'plen〕v. 抱怨
 again〔ə'gɛn〕adv. 再一次
 awfully〔'ɔfulɪ〕adv. 非常地
 cute〔kjut〕adj. 可愛的　　try〔traɪ〕v. 試著
 quiet〔'kwaɪət〕adj. 安靜的 (比較級用 more ～或-er 均可)
 maybe〔'mebɪ〕adv. 可能；或許
 should〔ʃud〕aux. 應該　　get〔gɛt〕v. 買
 fence〔fɛns〕n. 籬笆；圍牆

17. (**A**) How about doughnuts for breakfast?

A. That sounds great.

B. No, I always eat breakfast.

C. You don't need to lose weight.

* ***How about~?*** ~如何；~怎麼樣？
  doughnut (ˈdoˌnʌt) *n.* 甜甜圈 (= *donut*)
  breakfast (ˈbrɛkfəst) *n.* 早餐
  sound (saʊnd) *v.* 聽起來
  great (gret) *adj.* 很棒的
  That sounds great. 那聽起來很棒。
  always (ˈɔlwez) *adv.* 總是
  need (nid) *v.* 需要　　lose (luz) *v.* 減少
  weight (wet) *n.* 體重　　***lose weight*** 減肥

18. (**C**) Do you exercise every day?

A. Yes. I always finish my homework.

B. Yes, I'm an optimistic person.

C. No. I work out only twice a week.

* exercise (ˈɛksəˌsaɪz) *v.* 運動
  finish (ˈfɪnɪʃ) *v.* 完成；做完
  homework (ˈhomˌwɝk) *n.* 家庭作業
  optimistic (ˌɑptəˈmɪstɪk) *adj.* 樂觀的
  person (ˈpɝsn̩) *n.* 人　　***work out*** 運動
  only (ˈonlɪ) *adv.* 只有
  twice (twaɪs) *adv.* 兩次

19. (**B**) What time does the museum open?

    A. Until 7:00.

    B. At 9 a.m., Tuesday through Sunday.

    C. Yes, it is.

    * ***what time*** 幾點   museum〔mju'ziəm〕*n.* 博物館

       open〔'opən〕*v.* 開門

       until〔ən'tɪl〕*prep.* 直到…為止

       a.m.〔'e'εm〕*adj.* 早上（*p.m.* 下午）

       Tuesday〔'tjuzde, -dɪ〕*n.* 星期二

       through〔θru〕*prep.*（從…）到～

       Sunday〔'sʌnde, -dɪ〕*n.* 星期日

20. (**A**) Didn't you hear me calling you?

    A. No. I was on the balcony.

    B. Yes, I didn't. Sorry.

    C. No, I won't be here tomorrow.

    * hear〔hɪr〕*v.* 聽見   call〔kɔl〕*v.* 叫喚

       balcony〔'bælkənɪ〕*n.* 陽台

       sorry〔'sɔrɪ〕*interj.* 對不起

       won't〔wont〕將不…（= *will not*）

       here〔hɪr〕*adv.* 在這裡

第三部份

21. (**A**) M：You sure have a lot of textbooks.

    W：That's because I'm taking six subjects.

    M：Were they expensive?

    W：No, they're supplied by the school.

Question：Why does the woman have so many books?

A. She is taking a lot of subjects.

B. They are supplied by the school.

C. They are too expensive to leave behind.

* sure〔ʃʊr〕*adv.* 的確　　*a lot of* ~　許多~
textbook〔'tɛkst,bʊk〕*n.* 教科書
because〔bɪ'kɔz〕*conj.* 因為　　take〔tek〕*v.* 修（課）
subject〔'sʌbdʒɪkt〕*n.* 科目
expensive〔ɪk'spɛnsɪv〕*adj.* 昂貴的
supply〔sə'plaɪ〕*v.* 供應　　so〔so〕*adv.* 如此地
too…to ~　太…以致不能~　　leave〔liv〕*v.* 留下
behind〔bɪ'haɪnd〕*adv.* 留在後面
leave behind 遺落；忘記帶

22. (**A**) M：I hear you have Ms. Jefferson for English.

W：Yes, and I'm really worried.

M：Why?

W：I've heard she's very hard to please.

Question：What is Ms. Jefferson like?

A. She is strict.　　B. She is worried.

C. She doesn't like to answer questions.

* hear〔hɪr〕*v.* 聽說
Ms.〔mɪz〕*n.* ~女士（不知女性是否已婚時，加在其姓或名之前）
really〔'rɪəlɪ〕*adv.* 真地　　worried〔'wɜɪd〕*adj.* 擔心的
hard to V. 難以~的　　please〔pliz〕*v.* 取悅；使高興
like〔laɪk〕*prep.* 像　*v.* 喜歡
What is sb. like? ~是個怎麼樣的人？
strict〔strɪkt〕*adj.* 嚴厲的　　answer〔'ænsə〕*v.* 回答

23. (**C**) M：Are you going to ask Anna to come mountain climbing with us?

W：I'll ask her, but she fears heights.

M：I didn't know that.

Question：What didn't the man know?

A. Whether or not he will go mountain climbing.

B. That the woman is afraid to ask Anna.

C. That Anna is afraid of high places.

* ***mountain climbing*** 登山　　fear〔 fɪr 〕*v.* 害怕
heights〔 haɪts 〕*n. pl.* 高處　　whether〔'hwɛðɚ 〕*conj.* 是否
whether or not 是否　　afraid〔 ə'fred 〕*adj.* 害怕的
be afraid of~ 害怕~　　high〔 haɪ 〕*adj.* 高的

24. (**B**) M：Do you know the population of Beijing?

W：No, but I know it's one of the biggest cities in Asia.

M：And more people are moving there every day.

Question：What do they say about Beijing?

A. It is the biggest city in the world.

B. Beijing has a large population.

C. Beijing is a very polluted city.

* population〔,pɑjə'leʃən 〕*n.* 人口
Beijing〔'be'dʒɪŋ 〕*n.* 北京　　***one of***~ ~其中之一
biggest〔'bɪgɪst 〕*adj.* 最大的（ big 的最高級）
Asia〔'eʃə 〕*n.* 亞洲　　more〔 mor 〕*adj.* 更多的
move〔 muv 〕*v.* 遷移；搬家　　world〔 wɝld 〕*n.* 世界
a large population 很多人口
polluted〔 pə'lutɪd 〕*adj.* 受污染的

25. (**A**)　M：Wow.　Your nose is really red.

W：That's because I went golfing today.

M：You should have worn a cap.

Question：What would have happened if the woman

had worn a cap?

A.　She would not have gotten sunburned.

B.　She would have played better.

C.　She wouldn't be black.

* wow〔waʊ〕*interj.* 哇；噢（表示驚訝等的叫聲）

nose〔noz〕*n.* 鼻子　　golf〔gɔlf, gɑlf〕*v.* 打高爾夫球

should have + ***p.p.*** 當初應該（表過去該做而未做）

wear〔wɛr〕*v.* 穿；戴（三態變化為：wear-wore-worn）

cap〔kæp〕*n.* （無邊的）帽子

happen〔'hæpən〕*v.* 發生　　***get*** + ***p.p.*** 成為…狀態

sunburned〔'sʌn,bɜnd〕*adj.* 曬傷的

would have + ***p.p.*** 過去可能已經…（表與過去事實相反）

play〔ple〕*v.* 打（球）

better〔'bɛtɚ〕*adv.* 更好地（well 的比較級）

26. (**B**)　M：Are these medicines the same?

W：Yes, but one is in the form of a pill and the other is

a powder.

M：How do I take the powder?

W：You mix 2 grams with exactly 50 milliliters of water.

M：That sounds like too much trouble.

Question：Which medicine will the man buy?

A. He will buy 2 grams of medicine.

B. He will buy the pills.

C. He will buy the liquid medicine.

* medicine〔'mɛdəsn̩〕n. 藥　　***the same*** 相同的
  form〔fɔrm〕n. 形式　　***in the form of***~ 以~的形式
  pill〔pɪl〕n. 藥丸　　***the other*** 其餘的（物）
  powder〔'paʊdɚ〕n. 粉；粉末　　take〔tek〕v. 吃（藥）
  mix〔mɪks〕v. 混合　　gram〔græm〕n. 公克
  exactly〔ɪg'zæktlɪ〕adv. 剛好
  milliliter〔'mɪlə,litɚ〕n. 毫升（= ml）
  sound like 聽起來像　　trouble〔'trʌbl̩〕n. 麻煩
  which〔hwɪtʃ〕adj. 哪一個　　liquid〔'lɪkwɪd〕adj. 液體的

27.（ **C** ）M : What time does the bus leave?

W : A bus leaves every hour on the hour.

M : Okay. I'll take a ticket for the seven o'clock bus.

W : A.M. or P.M.?

M : P.M.

Question : When will the man leave?

A. Every hour on the hour.

B. At seven in the morning.　　C. In the evening.

* leave〔liv〕v. 離開；出發　　hour〔aʊr〕n. 一小時
  every hour on the hour 每個整點（= ***on the hour***）
  okay〔'o'ke〕adv. 好（= ***OK***）　　take〔tek〕v. 買
  ticket〔'tɪkɪt〕n. 車票　　A.M.〔'e'ɛm〕adv. 早上（= ***a.m.***）
  P.M.〔'pi'ɛm〕adv. 下午（= ***p.m.***）
  evening〔'ivnɪŋ〕n. 傍晚

28. (**C**) M : This chair is uncomfortable.

W : It's probably too low for you.

M : Can I change it?

W : Sure. Just turn this handle.

Question : What does the woman suggest the man do?

A. Change his seat to another chair.

B. Turn his chair around.

C. Raise his chair.

* chair〔tʃɛr〕*n.* 椅子

uncomfortable〔ʌnˈkʌmfɚtəbḷ〕*adj.* 不舒服的

probably〔ˈprɑbəblɪ〕*adv.* 可能　　low〔lo〕*adj.* 低的

change〔tʃendʒ〕*v.* 改變　　sure〔ʃʊr〕*adv.* 當然

just〔dʒʌst〕*adv.* 就⋯（委婉的祈使語氣）

turn〔tɜn〕*v.* 轉　　handle〔ˈhændḷ〕*n.* 手把

suggest〔səgˈdʒɛst〕*v.* 建議　　seat〔sit〕*n.* 座位

another〔əˈnʌðɚ〕*adj.* 另一個　　***turn around*** 旋轉

raise〔rez〕*v.* 提高

29. (**A**) M : Where is your mother?

W : She went to the hairdresser.

M : Again? She went just last week.

Question : What is the man complaining about?

A. His wife spends too much time at the beauty salon.

B. His wife spends too much money on clothes.

C. His wife had promised to go to the hairdresser

last week.

* hairdresser〔'hɛr͵drɛsə〕n. 美髮師

again〔ə'gɛn〕adv. 又；再　　just〔dʒʌst〕adv. 才

last week 上個星期　　complain〔kəm'plen〕v. 抱怨

complain about~ 抱怨~　　wife〔waɪf〕n. 妻子

spend〔spɛnd〕v. 花（時間、金錢）

salon〔sə'lɑn〕n. 沙龍　　*beauty salon* 美容院

clothes〔kloðz〕n. pl. 衣服

promise〔'pramɪs〕v. 答應；保證

30.（**C**）M：I hear you climbed that mountain yesterday.

W：Yes, but it's really more of a hill.

M：It's still an accomplishment.

Question：What does the woman say about her climb?

A. She did not accomplish her goal.

B. She would like to climb more hills.

C. She did not climb very high.

* hear〔hɪr〕v. 聽說　　climb〔klaɪm〕v. 爬　n. 攀登

mountain〔'maʊntn̩〕n. 山　　really〔'riəlɪ〕adv. 真地

more of 更大程度上的　　hill〔hɪl〕n. 山丘

more of a hill 比山丘高一點　　still〔stɪl〕adv. 仍然

accomplishment〔ə'kamplɪʃmənt〕n. 成就

accomplish〔ə'kamplɪʃ〕v. 完成；達成

goal〔gol〕n. 目標

would like to V. 想要~（= *want to V.*）

more〔mor〕adj. 更多的　　high〔haɪ〕adv. 高地

全民英語能力分級檢定測驗

初級測驗⑥

　　本測驗分三部份，全為三選一之選擇題，每部份各 10 題，共 30
題，作答時間約 20 分鐘。

第一部份：看圖辨義

　　　　　本部份共 10 題，試題冊上每題有一個圖片，請聽錄音機
　　　　　播出一個相關的問題，與 A、B、C 三個英語敘述後，選
　　　　　一個與所看到圖片最相符的答案，並在答案紙上相對的圓
　　　　　圈內塗黑作答。每題播出一遍，問題及選項均不印在試題
　　　　　冊上。

例：（看）

（聽）

Look at the picture. How
much is the hamburger?

　　A. It's eighty dollars.
　　B. It's fifty-five dollars.
　　C. It's eighteen dollars.

正確答案為 A

A. **Question 1**

B. **Question 2**

C. <u>Question 3</u>

D. <u>Question 4</u>

請 翻 頁 ⟹

E. <u>Question 5</u>

F. <u>Question 6</u>

G. <u>Question 7</u>

H. Question 8

I. Questions 9-10

請翻頁 ⇨

第二部份： 問答

本部份共10題，每題錄音機會播出一個問句或直述句，每題播出一次，聽後請從試題冊上 A、B、C 三個選項中，選出一個最適合的回答或回應，並在答案紙上塗黑作答。

例：

（聽） Good morning, Kevin. How are you?

（看） A. I'm fine, thank you.
B. I'm in the living room.
C. My name is Kevin.

正確答案為 A

11. A. I've never been there.
B. It's delicious.
C. Sure. I think it's smart and humorous.

12. A. Here you are.
B. But I do love bread.
C. You shouldn't just sit around.

13. A. It starts on January 20th.
B. I'm going to California with my family.
C. Yes, we always have a winter vacation.

14. A. No, you mustn't.
B. Yes, it's not.
C. You don't have to.

15. A. Yes, just one table.
    B. No. I'm expecting a guest.
    C. I'd rather not.

16. A. That's my dream.
    B. If the weather is nice, why not?
    C. Yes, I often do.

17. A. Yes. She's down to 50 kilograms.
    B. No, she's much happier now.
    C. She's gained a little weight.

18. A. Here. Give it to me.
    B. Your hair looks fine to me.
    C. Would you like some medicine?

19. A. Yes, next Saturday.
    B. No, she's still single.
    C. She hasn't decided yet.

20. A. All girls love their daddy.
    B. Why don't you make some?
    C. Yes, thank you.

請 翻 頁 ⟹

第三部份: 簡短對話

本部份共 10 題,每題錄音機會播出一段對話及一個相關
的問題,每題播出兩次,聽後請從試題冊上 A、B、C 三
個選項中,選出一個最適合的回答,並在答案紙上塗黑
作答。

例:

(聽)(Woman) Good afternoon, …Mr. Davis?

(Man) Yes. I have an appointment with
Dr. Sanders at two o'clock. My
son Tommy has a fever.

(Woman) Oh, that's too bad. Well, please
have a seat, Mr. Davis. Dr.
Sanders will be right with you.

Question: Where did this conversation take
place?

(看) A. In a post office.
B. In a restaurant.
C. In a doctor's office.

正確答案為 C

21. A. She sometimes gets
       sick when she goes
       home.
    B. Talking to her
       family makes her
       feel less lonely.
    C. She feels that living
       away from home is
       better.

22. A. She goes for
       business.
    B. Whenever she has
       free time.
    C. Three times per
       year.

23. A. It is very crowded on
       Saturday and Sunday.
    B. The museum is very
       popular because of its
       excellent view.
    C. Over 1000 people went
       there to meet Picasso.

24. A. Who cut the woman's
       hair.
    B. Where the woman cut
       herself.
    C. How the woman did it.

25. A. Their hobbies.
    B. The news.
    C. Their habits.

請 翻 頁 ⟹

26. A. She feels it was not a
    good birthday gift.
    B. She thinks she does
    not play it well.
    C. She believes she
    should have paid for
    it herself.

27. A. She is putting some
    books away.
    B. She writes books.
    C. She is a librarian.

28. A. He will place the gift
    around the woman's
    neck.
    B. He will help the
    woman return the gift.
    C. He will put the gift
    back in the box.

29. A. Stop taking the dog
    for walks on muddy
    days.
    B. Clean her shoes
    before going inside.
    C. Wipe the dog's feet
    after she walks him.

30. A. No, because the
    weather was bad.
    B. She had a good
    time despite the
    weather.
    C. No. She was bored
    with the museums
    and shops.

初級英語聽力檢定⑥詳解

第一部份

For question number 1, please look at picture A.

1. (**B**) Is the woman angry with the cat?
    A. Because it stole the fish.
    B. Yes, she is.
    C. She will hit it.

    * **be angry with**… 生…的氣　because〔bɪˋkɔz〕*conj.* 因為
    steal〔stil〕*v.* 偷（三態變化為：steal-stole-stolen）
    fish〔fɪʃ〕*n.* 魚　　hit〔hɪt〕*v.* 打

For question number 2, please look at picture B.

2. (**B**) Who is the man calling?
    A. A sausage.　　　B. A waiter.
    C. His breakfast.

    * call〔kɔl〕*v.* 叫喚　sausage〔ˋsɔsɪdʒ〕*n.* 香腸
    waiter〔ˋwetɚ〕*n.* 服務生　breakfast〔ˋbrɛkfəst〕*n.* 早餐

For question number 3, please look at picture C.

3. (**B**) What is bothering the man?
    A. He is eating lunch.
    B. There are some flies.
    C. He is frightened.

    * bother〔ˋbɑðɚ〕*v.* 打擾　lunch〔lʌntʃ〕*n.* 午餐
    fly〔flaɪ〕*n.* 蒼蠅　frightened〔ˋfraɪtṇd〕*adj.* 害怕的

For question number 4, please look at picture D.

4. (**C**) Where is the boy?

      A. He is brave.

      B. Yes, it is a tree.

      C. In the tree.

      * brave〔brev〕*adj.* 勇敢的　　tree〔tri〕*n.* 樹

For question number 5, please look at picture E.

5. (**A**) What did the boy do?

      A. He gave up his seat.

      B. He is on the train.

      C. Yes, he did it.

      * ***give up*** 放棄　　seat〔sit〕*n.* 座位

      give up *one's seat* 讓位

      train〔tren〕*n.* 火車

For question number 6, please look at picture F.

6. (**A**) Who was hit?

      A. A boy was.

      B. By a bicycle.

      C. Because he was careless.

      * hit〔hɪt〕*v.* 撞到（三態同形）

      bicycle〔'baɪsɪkl̩〕*n.* 腳踏車（= *bike*）

      careless〔'kɛrlɪs〕*adj.* 粗心的；不小心的

For question number 7, please look at picture G.

7. (**B**)　Why is the girl waving her hands?

  A.　She is leaving.

  B.　Insects are biting her.

  C.　Yes, she is.

  * wave〔wev〕v. 揮動　　hand〔hænd〕n. 手

   leave〔liv〕v. 離開　　insect〔'ɪnsɛkt〕n. 昆蟲

   bite〔baɪt〕v. 咬（三態變化爲：bite-bit-bitten）

For question number 8, please look at picture H.

8. (**C**)　What is this?

  A.　It is May 20th.

  B.　They are graduating.

  C.　It's a poster.

  * May〔me〕n. 五月　　graduate〔'grædʒu,et〕v. 畢業

   poster〔'postɚ〕n. 海報

For questions number 9 and 10, please look at picture I.

9. (**C**)　How many are in the group?

  A.　They are happy.

  B.　It's a basketball team.

  C.　There are seven.

  * group〔grup〕n. 團體

   basketball〔'bæskɪt,bɔl〕n. 籃球

   team〔tim〕n. 隊

10. (**C**)　Please look at picture I again. Who is standing right behind Sam?

   A. No, Tom is sitting. B. Yes, they are.

   C. Sean is.

   * right〔rɪt〕 *adv.* 正好 behind〔bɪˋhaɪnd〕*prep.* 在⋯後面

第二部份

11. (**B**)　Do you like cabbage?

   A. I've never been there.

   B. It's delicious.

   C. Sure. I think it's smart and humorous.

   * cabbage〔ˋkæbɪdʒ〕 *n.* 包心菜 ***have never been***　從未

   there〔ðɛr〕 *adv.* 往那裡；在那裡

   delicious〔dɪˋlɪʃəs〕 *adj.* 美味的

   sure〔ʃʊr〕 *adv.* 好；當然

   think〔θɪŋk〕 *v.* 認為（三態變化為：think-thought-thought）

   smart〔smɑrt〕 *adj.* 聰明的

   humorous〔ˋhjumərəs〕 *adj.* 幽默的

12. (**A**)　I'd like two loaves of bread.

   A. Here you are. B. But I do love bread.

   C. You shouldn't just sit around.

   * ***would like***　想要（ = *want* ） loaf〔lof〕 *n.* 一條（麵包）

   bread〔brɛd〕 *n.* 麵包

   Here you are. 你要的東西在這裡；拿去吧。（ = *Here it is.* ）

   do〔du〕 *aux.* 真的；的確（加強動詞的語氣）

   just〔dʒʌst〕 *adv.* 只是 ***sit around***　無所事事

13. (**B**) Do you have any plans for the winter vacation?

A. It starts on January 20th.

B. I'm going to California with my family.

C. Yes, we always have a winter vacation.

* plan〔plæn〕*n.* 計劃　　winter〔'wɪntɚ〕*n.* 冬天
vacation〔ve'keʃən〕*n.* 假期　***winter vacation*** 寒假
start〔stɑrt〕*v.* 開始　　January〔'dʒænjʊ,ɛrɪ〕*n.* 一月
California〔,kælə'fɔrnjə〕*n.* 加州
family〔'fæməlɪ〕*n.* 家人　　always〔'ɔlwez〕*adv.* 總是

14. (**C**) Is it necessary to finish this assignment today?

A. No, you mustn't.

B. Yes, it's not.

C. You don't have to.

* necessary〔'nɛsə,sɛrɪ〕*adj.* 必需的
finish〔'fɪnɪʃ〕*v.* 完成
assignment〔ə'saɪnmənt〕*n.* 功課
must〔mʌst〕*aux.* 一定；必須
mustn't + V. 絕對不能~　　***have to*** 必須

15. (**B**) A table for one?

A. Yes, just one table.

B. No. I'm expecting a guest.

C. I'd rather not.

* ***A table for one?*** 一個人用餐嗎？（餐廳服務生詢問）
expect〔ɪk'spɛkt〕*v.* 期待；等待
guest〔gɛst〕*n.* 客人
would rather not + V. 寧願不~

16. (**A**) Would you like to visit outer space?
      A. That's my dream.
      B. If the weather is nice, why not?
      C. Yes, I often do.

    * ***Would you like to V. ~ ?*** 你想要~嗎？
      visit〔'vɪzɪt〕v. 拜訪；遊覽   ***outer space*** 外太空
      dream〔drim〕n. 夢想   weather〔'wɛðɚ〕n. 天氣
      Why not? 爲什麼不去？   often〔'ɔfən〕adv. 經常

17. (**C**) Has Jessica gotten heavier?
      A. Yes. She's down to 50 kilograms.
      B. No, she's much happier now.
      C. She's gained a little weight.

    * get〔gɛt〕v. 變得
      heavier〔'hɛvɪɚ〕adj. 較重的（heavy 的比較級）
      down〔daʊn〕adv.（體重）下降
      kilogram〔'kɪlə,græm〕n. 公斤
      much〔mʌtʃ〕adv. 非常（可修飾比較級）
      happier〔'hæpɪɚ〕adj. 較高興的（happy 的比較級）
      gain〔gen〕v. 增加   weight〔wet〕n. 體重

18. (**C**) I wish this headache would go away.
      A. Here. Give it to me.
      B. Your hair looks fine to me.
      C. Would you like some medicine?

    * wish〔wɪʃ〕v. 希望   headache〔'hɛd,ek〕n. 頭痛
      go away 消失   here〔hɪr〕interj. 喂（用於引起注意）
      give〔gɪv〕v. 給   hair〔hɛr〕n. 頭髮
      look fine 看起來很好   medicine〔'mɛdəsn̩〕n. 藥

19. (**B**) Is your sister married?

A. Yes, next Saturday.

B. No, she's still single.

C. She hasn't decided yet.

* sister〔ˈsɪstɚ〕 *n.* 姊妹
　married〔ˈmærɪd〕 *adj.* 結婚的；已婚的
　next〔nɛkst〕 *adj.* 下一個
　Saturday〔ˈsætɚde, -dɪ〕 *n.* 星期六
　still〔stɪl〕 *adv.* 仍然　　single〔ˈsɪŋgl〕 *adj.* 單身的
　decide〔dɪˈsaɪd〕 *v.* 決定
　yet〔jɛt〕 *adv.* 尚（未）（用於否定句）

20. (**B**) I'd love some popcorn.

A. All girls love their daddy.

B. Why don't you make some?

C. Yes, thank you.

* *would love* 想要（= *would like*）
　popcorn〔ˈpɑpˌkɔrn〕 *n.* 爆米花
　love〔lʌv〕 *v.* 愛　　daddy〔ˈdædɪ〕 *n.* 爸爸
　make〔mek〕 *v.* 做　　some〔sʌm〕 *pron.* 一些

第三部份

21. (**B**) M：Do you ever get homesick?

W：Sometimes.

M：What do you do about it?

W：I call my family and then I feel better.

Question：What did the woman say?

A. She sometimes gets sick when she goes home.

B. Talking to her family makes her feel less lonely.

C. She feels that living away from home is better.

* ever〔ˋɛvɚ〕*adv.* 曾經　　***get homesick*** 想家
  sometimes〔ˋsʌm͵taɪmz〕*adv.* 有時候
  do about 處理；應付　　call〔kɔl〕*v.* 打電話給～
  and then 然後　　***feel better*** 覺得好一點
  get sick 生病　　***talk to***～ 和～說話
  make〔mek〕*v.* 使　　less〔lɛs〕*adv.* 較不
  lonely〔ˋlonlɪ〕*adj.* 寂寞的　　***away from***～ 遠離～
  better〔ˋbɛtɚ〕*adj.* 較好的

22. (**C**) M：Do you travel a lot for business?

W：Yes.　I go to Italy three times yearly.

M：That must be fun.

W：Yes.　I usually have a little free time while I'm there.

Question：When does the woman go to Italy?

A. She goes for business.

B. Whenever she has free time.

C. Three times per year.

* travel〔ˋtrævl̩〕*v.* 旅行　　***a lot*** 常常（作副詞用）
  business〔ˋbɪznɪs〕*n.* 工作　　Italy〔ˋɪtl̩ɪ〕*n.* 義大利
  time〔taɪm〕*n.* 次數　　yearly〔ˋjɪrlɪ〕*adv.* 每年
  must〔mʌst〕*aux.* 一定　　fun〔fʌn〕*adj.* 有趣的；好玩的
  usually〔ˋjuʒʊəlɪ〕*adv.* 通常　　***a little*** 一點
  free〔fri〕*adj.* 空閒的　　while〔hwaɪl〕*conj.* 當…的時候
  whenever〔hwɛnˋɛvɚ〕*adv.* 無論何時
  per〔pɚ〕*prep.* 每…

23. (**A**)　M：Are you going to the Picasso exhibition?

　　　　W：I went last Sunday.

　　　　M：How was it?

　　　　W：Very popular.　At least 1000 people view the exhibition every weekend.

　　　Question：What does the woman say about the museum?

　　A.　It is very crowded on Saturday and Sunday.

　　B.　The museum is very popular because of its excellent view.

　　C.　Over 1000 people went there to meet Picasso.

* Picasso〔pɪˋkɑso〕*n.* 畢卡索

　exhibition〔͵ɛksəˋbɪʃən〕*n.* 展覽

　Sunday〔ˋsʌnde, -dɪ〕*n.* 星期日

　last Sunday 上星期日

　popular〔ˋpɑpjələ〕*adj.* 受歡迎的

　at least 至少　　view〔vju〕*v.* 看　*n.* 風景

　weekend〔ˋwikˋɛnd〕*n.* 週末

　museum〔mjuˋziəm〕*n.* 博物館

　crowded〔ˋkraʊdɪd〕*adj.* 擁擠的

　because of (+N. or V-ing) 因為⋯

　excellent〔ˋɛkslənt〕*adj.* 極好的

　over〔ˋovə〕*prep.* 超過 (= *more than*)

　meet〔mit〕*v.* 和⋯見面 (三態變化為：meet-met-met)

24. (**A**)　M：Did you get a haircut?

　　　　　　W：Yes.　Do you like it?

　　　　　　M：Yeah.　Where did you have it done?

　　　　Question：What does the man want to know?

　　　　A. Who cut the woman's hair.

　　　　B. Where the woman cut herself.

　　　　C. How the woman did it.

　　　　* haircut〔'hɛr͵kʌt〕*n.* 理髮

　　　　　get a haircut 去理髮（= *have a haircut*）

　　　　　like〔laɪk〕*v.* 喜歡

　　　　　yeah〔jæ〕*adv.* 是的（= *yes*）

　　　　　have + N. + p.p. 使…成（～的狀態）

　　　　　want〔wɑnt〕*v.* 想要　　hair〔hɛr〕*n.* 頭髮

　　　　　cut〔kʌt〕*v.* 剪；割傷

25. (**C**)　M：Do you usually drink coffee in the morning?

　　　　　　W：Yes.　I always have a cup while I read the
　　　　　　　　newspaper.

　　　　　　M：I don't usually read the newspaper, but I often
　　　　　　　　watch the TV news in the morning.

　　　　Question：What are they talking about?

　　　　A. Their hobbies.

　　　　B. The news.

　　　　C. Their habits.

* drink〔drɪŋk〕v. 喝　　coffee〔'kɔfɪ〕n. 咖啡

  have〔hæv〕v. 吃；喝　　cup〔kʌp〕n. 杯

  while〔hwaɪl〕conj. 當…的時候　　read〔rid〕v. 讀

  newspaper〔'njuz,pepɚ〕n. 報紙

  watch〔wɑtʃ〕v. 看（電視）　　news〔njuz〕n. 新聞

  talk about 談論　　hobby〔'hɑbɪ〕n. 嗜好

  habit〔'hæbɪt〕n. 習慣

26. (**B**) M：What did your parents give you for your birthday?

  W：They gave me a flute.

  M：That's a nice gift.

  W：Yes, but I wish I could play better.

  Question：How does the woman feel about the flute?

  A. She feels it was not a good birthday gift.

  B. She thinks she does not play it well.

  C. She believes she should have paid for it herself.

* parents〔'pɛrənts〕n. pl. 父母

  flute〔flut〕n. 笛子　　nice〔naɪs〕adj. 好的

  gift〔gɪft〕n. 禮物　　wish〔wɪʃ〕v. 希望

  could〔kʊd〕aux. 能（在此為「與現在事實相反」的假設法）

  play〔ple〕v. 演奏　　better〔'bɛtɚ〕adv. 更好

  feel〔fil〕v. 覺得　　well〔wɛl〕adv. 好地

  believe〔bɪ'liv〕v. 認為；相信

  should have + *p.p.* 當初應該（表過去該做而未做）

  pay for～　付～的錢

  herself〔hɚ'sɛlf〕pron. 她自己（加強語氣的用法）

27. (**C**)　M：Do you enjoy organizing things?

W：No, not really.

M：Then why are you putting these books back on the shelves?

W：It's my job.

Question：What does the woman do?

A. She is putting some books away.

B. She writes books.

C. She is a librarian.

* enjoy〔 ɪn'dʒɔɪ 〕*v.* 喜歡；享受

organize〔'ɔrgən,aɪz 〕*v.* 整理；組織

not really　不完全是

then〔 ðɛn 〕*adv.* 那麼　　put〔 pʊt 〕*v.* 放

back〔 bæk 〕*adv.* 返回

shelf〔 ʃɛlf 〕*n.* 架子（複數為 shelves〔 ʃɛlvz 〕）

job〔 dʒɑb 〕*n.* 工作

What does the woman do?　這女生的職業是什麼？

put away　收拾

librarian〔 laɪ'brɛrɪən 〕*n.* 圖書館員

28. (**A**)　M：Here is a gift for you.

W：What a beautiful necklace. You shouldn't have.

M：Let me help you put it on.

Question：What will the man do?

A. He will place the gift around the woman's neck.

B. He will help the woman return the gift.

C. He will put the gift back in the box.

* *Here is*～. 這是～。
  what〔hwɑt〕*adj.* 多麼的【用於感嘆句，放在名詞（片語）前】
  beautiful〔'bjutəfəl〕*adj.* 美麗的
  necklace〔'nɛklɪs〕*n.* 項鍊
  shouldn't have + *p.p.* 當初不該～（表過去不該做而已做）
  help〔hɛlp〕*v.* 幫助　　*put on* 戴上
  place〔ples〕*v.* 放置　　around〔ə'raʊnd〕*prep.* 圍繞
  neck〔nɛk〕*n.* 脖子　　return〔rɪ'tɜn〕*v.* 歸還

29. (**B**) M：Where did all this mud come from?

W：I took the dog for a walk.

M：I wish you would remember to wipe your feet
　　before you come in.

Question：What should the woman do?

A. Stop taking the dog for walks on muddy days.

B. Clean her shoes before going inside.

C. Wipe the dog's feet after she walks him.

* mud〔mʌd〕*n.* 泥巴　　*come from*～ 來自～
  take〔tek〕*v.* 帶　　walk〔wɔk〕*n.* 散步
  would〔wʊd〕*aux.* 會（在此為「與現在事實相反」的假設法）
  remember〔rɪ'mɛmbə〕*v.* 記得
  wipe〔waɪp〕*v.* 擦　　feet〔fit〕*n. pl.* 腳（foot 的複數）
  come in 進來　　*stop* + *V-ing* 停止～
  muddy〔'mʌdɪ〕*adj.* 泥濘的　　days〔dez〕*n. pl.* 日子
  clean〔klin〕*v.* 清理　　shoes〔ʃuz〕*n. pl.* 鞋子
  inside〔'ɪn'saɪd〕*adv.* 向屋內

30. (**B**)　M：How was the weather during your trip?

W：It was bad, but we had fun anyway.

M：What did you do?

W：We visited some museums and went shopping.

Question：Did the woman enjoy her vacation?

A. No, because the weather was bad.

B. She had a good time despite the weather.

C. No.　She was bored with the museums and shops.

* weather〔'wɛðɚ〕*n.* 天氣

during〔'djurɪŋ〕*prep.* 在…期間

trip〔trɪp〕*n.* 旅行　　bad〔bæd〕*adj.* 不好的

have fun 玩得愉快　　anyway〔'ɛnɪ,we〕*adv.* 無論如何

What did you do? 你們做了什麼？

【不同於 *What <u>do</u> you do?*（你的職業是什麼？）】

visit〔'vɪzɪt〕*v.* 參觀；遊覽

museum〔mju'ziəm〕*n.* 博物館

shop〔ʃɑp〕*v.* 購物　　*n.* 商店

go shopping 去購物　　vacation〔ve'keʃən〕*n.* 假期

because〔bɪ'kɔz〕*conj.* 因為

have a good time 玩得愉快

despite〔dɪ'spaɪt〕*prep.* 不管；儘管

bored〔bord〕*adj.* 覺得無聊的；厭煩的

be bored with ~ 對~感到厭煩的

全民英語能力分級檢定測驗

初級測驗⑦

本測驗分三部份，全爲三選一之選擇題，每部份各 10 題，共 30 題，作答時間約 20 分鐘。

第一部份：看圖辨義

本部份共 10 題，試題冊上每題有一個圖片，請聽錄音機播出一個相關的問題，與 A、B、C 三個英語敘述後，選一個與所看到圖片最相符的答案，並在答案紙上相對的圓圈內塗黑作答。每題播出一遍，問題及選項均不印在試題冊上。

例：（看）

NT$80　NT$50

（聽）

Look at the picture. How much is the hamburger?

　　A. It's eighty dollars.
　　B. It's fifty-five dollars.
　　C. It's eighteen dollars.

正確答案爲 A

A. **Questions 1-2**

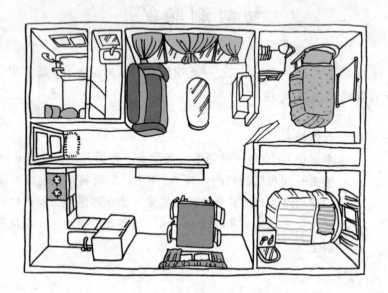

B. **Question 3**

Fred

C. __Question 4__

D. __Question 5__

E. __Question 6__

請 翻 頁 ⟹

F. <u>Question 7</u>

G. <u>Question 8</u>

H. **Question 9**

I. **Question 10**

請翻頁

第二部份： 問答

本部份共 10 題，每題錄音機會播出一個問句或直述句，
每題播出一次，聽後請從試題冊上 A、B、C 三個選項
中，選出一個最適合的回答或回應，並在答案紙上塗黑
作答。

例：

（聽） Good morning, Kevin. How are you?

（看） A. I'm fine, thank you.

B. I'm in the living room.

C. My name is Kevin.

正確答案為 A

11. A. Yes, I'm afraid there
   are.

B. Yes, I do.

C. I don't believe in them.

12. A. Don't insult me!

B. I feel dizzy.

C. Maybe I need glasses.

13. A. Tommy threw a
   baseball through it.

B. Yes, it's shut.

C. I just turned on the
   air conditioner.

14. A. All except for the last
       two pages.
    B. No, I haven't read all
       of the books.
    C. Yes. I'm reading it now.

15. A. Here you are.
    B. I'll write to you soon.
    C. Who is it from?

16. A. No one has ever
       drowned here.
    B. Yes. It's five meters at
       that end.
    C. Stay in the shallow water
       if you don't swim well.

17. A. It should be here at 6:15.
    B. It stops at Taichung
       and Taipei.
    C. It's the number 16 on
       platform 2.

18. A. Yes, my salary is
       too small.
    B. Yes, I play every
       week.
    C. Yes, on Fridays.

19. A. Thank you, they're
       delicious.
    B. I think you have
       three.
    C. Are they chocolate?

20. A. Unfortunately, he's
       very noisy.
    B. No, he's quite
       gentle.
    C. No, he's not very
       smart.

請 翻 頁 ⟹

第三部份： 簡短對話

本部份共 10 題，每題錄音機會播出一段對話及一個相關的問題，每題播出兩次，聽後請從試題冊上 A、B、C 三個選項中，選出一個最適合的回答，並在答案紙上塗黑作答。

例：

（聽）	(Woman)	Good afternoon, ...Mr. Davis?
	(Man)	Yes. I have an appointment with Dr. Sanders at two o'clock. My son Tommy has a fever.
	(Woman)	Oh, that's too bad. Well, please have a seat, Mr. Davis. Dr. Sanders will be right with you.

Question: Where did this conversation take place?

（看） A. In a post office.
B. In a restaurant.
C. In a doctor's office.

正確答案為 C

21. A. He will not thank
the woman for taking
out the trash.

B. He will take out the
trash while the
woman sweeps the
floor.

C. He would rather
sweep the floor than
take out the trash.

22. A. Some taxis.

B. The airport.

C. The man's luggage.

23. A. In the bathtub.

B. On the stairs.

C. On the fourth floor.

24. A. Go shopping for some
decorations.

B. Change to another
room.

C. Put some pictures on
the wall.

25. A. Buy smaller plants.

B. Cut down the big plants.

C. Put the plants into
bigger pots.

26. A. She gives him two
meals a day.

B. She gives him five
years.

C. She gives him only
dog food.

請 翻 頁 ⫸

27. A. The woman has neither
       a pen nor a pencil.
    B. The man prefers
       markers to pens and
       pencils.
    C. The man has a pen and
       a pencil, but no marker.

28. A. The woman bought a
       car for NT$1000
       yesterday.
    B. The woman borrowed
       the car for one day.
    C. The woman does not
       own a car.

29. A. Going to a game.
    B. Watching TV.
    C. Looking at the
       clock.

30. A. The boat is clean,
       but it is not
       comfortable.
    B. The boat will not
       move without
       wind.
    C. She does not want
       to get wet.

初級英語聽力檢定⑦詳解

第一部份

For questions number 1 and 2, please look at picture A.

1. (**C**) How many bedrooms are there?
    A. They are next to the windows.
    B. There are two beds.
    C. There are two of them.

    * bedroom〔'bɛd,rum〕*n.* 臥室　　***next to~*** 在~旁邊
    window〔'wɪndo〕*n.* 窗戶　　bed〔bɛd〕*n.* 床
    them〔ðɛm〕*pron.* 他們 (代替前已提及的 bedrooms 的受格)

2. (**A**) Please look at picture A again. How many people
    might live in this house?
    A. Two or three.　　B. Twelve people.
    C. There are no people in the house.

    * people〔'pipl̩〕*n. pl.* 人　　might〔maɪt〕*aux.* 可能
    live〔lɪv〕*v.* 住

For question number 3, please look at picture B.

3. (**B**) How is Fred eating his food?
    A. He is hungry.　　B. He is using a fork.
    C. He is eating spaghetti.

    * food〔fud〕*n.* 食物　　hungry〔'hʌŋgrɪ〕*adj.* 飢餓的
    use〔juz〕*v.* 使用　　fork〔fɔrk〕*n.* 叉子
    spaghetti〔spə'gɛtɪ〕*n.* 義大利麵

For question number 4, please look at picture C.

4. (**A**) What is on the cabinet?

    A. There are bats on it.

    B. There are two gloves on the shelf.

    C. There are two shelves.

    * cabinet〔'kæbənɪt〕*n.* 櫥櫃　　bat〔bæt〕*n.* 球棒
　　glove〔glʌv〕*n.* 手套
　　shelf〔ʃɛlf〕*n.* 架子（複數為 shelves〔ʃɛlvz〕）

For question number 5, please look at picture D.

5. (**C**) Is the car inside?

    A. Yes, it is inside the house.

    B. No, it is in a parking lot.

    C. Yes, it is in the garage.

    * inside〔'ɪn'saɪd〕*adv.* 在室內　〔ɪn'saɪd〕*prep.* 在…裡面
　　park〔pɑrk〕*v.* 停車　　*parking lot* 停車場
　　garage〔gə'rɑʒ〕*n.* 車庫

For question number 6, please look at picture E.

6. (**C**) What has been turned on?

    A. No, the pillow is not on the sofa.

    B. There is a picture on the wall.

    C. The TV is on.

    * *turn on* 打開（電器）　　pillow〔'pɪlo〕*n.* 枕頭
　　sofa〔'sofə〕*n.* 沙發　　picture〔'pɪktʃə〕*n.* 圖畫
　　wall〔wɔl〕*n.* 牆壁　　on〔ɑn〕*adv.* 開著

For question number 7, please look at picture F.

7. (**B**) What is the comic book like?

    A. Yes, she likes it.   B. It is very funny.

    C. It is a storybook.

    * like〔laɪk〕*prep.* 像 *v.* 喜歡

    What be ~like? ～怎麼樣？

    comic〔'kɑmɪk〕*adj.* 漫畫的   funny〔'fʌnɪ〕*adj.* 好笑的

    storybook〔'storɪ,bʊk〕*n.* 故事書

For question number 8, please look at picture G.

8. (**B**) What is the boy waiting for?

    A. He is waiting by the traffic light.

    B. For the light to turn green.

    C. With his dog.

    * ***wait for*** 等待   by〔baɪ〕*prep.* 在…旁邊

    traffic〔'træfɪk〕*n.* 交通   light〔laɪt〕*n.* 燈

    traffic light 紅綠燈   turn〔tɜn〕*v.* 變成

    green〔grin〕*adj.* 綠色的

For question number 9, please look at picture H.

9. (**A**) Which class is this?

    A. They are studying science.

    B. It is a junior high school.

    C. It is a cooking class.

    * which〔hwɪtʃ〕*adj.* 哪一個   class〔klæs〕*n.* 課程

    study〔'stʌdɪ〕*v.* 學習   science〔'saɪəns〕*n.* 科學

    junior high school 國中   cooking〔'kʊkɪŋ〕*n.* 烹飪

For question number 10, please look at picture I.

10. (**A**) What are the dogs searching for?

    A. They are looking for the cat.

    B. No, there are only two dogs.

    C. They want to find the tree.

    * search〔sɜtʃ〕*v.* 尋找 *<for>* **look for** 尋找
    find〔faɪnd〕*v.* 找

第二部份

11. (**C**) Are you afraid of ghosts?

    A. Yes, I'm afraid there are.

    B. Yes, I do.

    C. I don't believe in them.

    * ***be afraid of*** ~ 害怕~   ***I'm afraid*** ~ 恐怕~
    ghost〔gost〕*n.* 鬼   ***believe in*** ~ 相信~的存在

12. (**B**) You don't look well.

    A. Don't insult me!

    B. I feel dizzy.

    C. Maybe I need glasses.

    * ***look well*** 氣色看起來不錯
    insult〔'ɪnsʌlt〕*v.* 侮辱   feel〔fil〕*v.* 覺得
    dizzy〔'dɪzɪ〕*adj.* 頭暈的
    maybe〔'mebi〕*adv.* 可能；或許
    need〔nid〕*v.* 需要   glasses〔'glæsɪz〕*n. pl.* 眼鏡

13. (**C**) Why is the window shut?

    A. Tommy threw a baseball through it.

    B. Yes, it's shut.

    C. I just turned on the air conditioner.

    * shut〔ʃʌt〕v. 關閉（三態同形）

      throw〔θro〕v. 丟（三態變化為：throw-threw-thrown）

      baseball〔'bes,bɔl〕n. 棒球

      through〔θru〕prep. 穿過；通過

      just〔dʒʌst〕adv. 才；剛剛   ***turn on*** 打開（電器）

      air conditioner 空調系統；冷氣

14. (**A**) Have you read the entire book?

    A. All except for the last two pages.

    B. No, I haven't read all of the books.

    C. Yes. I'm reading it now.

    * read〔rid〕v. 讀（三態變化為：read-read〔rɛd〕-read〔rɛd〕）

      entire〔ɪn'taɪr〕adj. 全部的   ***except for*** ⋯⋯ 除⋯⋯以外

      last〔læst〕adj. 最後的   page〔pedʒ〕n. 頁

15. (**A**) Can you give me an envelope for my letter?

    A. Here you are.

    B. I'll write to you soon.

    C. Who is it from?

    * give〔gɪv〕v. 給   envelope〔'ɛnvə,lop〕n. 信封

      letter〔'lɛtɚ〕n. 信

      Here you are. 你要的東西在這裡；拿去吧。(= *Here it is.*)

      write to sb. 寫信給某人   soon〔sun〕adv. 馬上；很快地

      Who is it from? 誰寄來的？

16. (**B**) Is this pool deep enough for diving?

    A. No one has ever drowned here.

    B. Yes.　It's five meters at that end.

    C. Stay in the shallow water if you don't swim well.

  * pool〔pul〕*n.* 游泳池　　deep〔dip〕*adj.* 深的
    enough〔ə'nʌf〕*adv.* 足夠地
    dive〔daɪv〕*v.* 跳水　　ever〔'ɛvɚ〕*adv.* 曾經
    drown〔draʊn〕*v.* 淹死　　meter〔'mitɚ〕*n.* 公尺
    end〔ɛnd〕*n.* 一端　　stay〔ste〕*v.* 停留
    shallow〔'ʃælo〕*adj.* 淺的
    swim〔swɪm〕*v.* 游泳　　well〔wɛl〕*adv.* 良好地

17. (**A**) When will the train arrive at the station?

    A. It should be here at 6:15.

    B. It stops at Taichung and Taipei.

    C. It's the number 16 on platform 2.

  * train〔tren〕*n.* 火車　　arrive〔ə'raɪv〕*v.* 抵達
    station〔'steʃən〕*n.* 車站
    should〔ʃʊd〕*aux.* 應該　　here〔hɪr〕*adv.* 到這裡
    stop〔stɑp〕*v.* 停車 < *at* >
    Taichung〔'taɪ'tʃʊŋ〕*n.* 台中
    Taipei〔'taɪ'pe〕*n.* 台北
    number〔'nʌmbɚ〕*n.* 第～號
    platform〔'plæt,fɔrm〕*n.* 月台

18. (**C**) Are you paid weekly?

    A. Yes, my salary is too small.

    B. Yes, I play every week.

    C. Yes, on Fridays.

    * pay〔pe〕v. 支付（薪水）
    weekly〔'wiklɪ〕adv. 每週
    salary〔'sælərɪ〕n. 薪水　　small〔smɔl〕adj. 少的
    Friday〔'fraɪde, -dɪ〕n. 星期五

19. (**B**) Can you guess how many cookies I have?

    A. Thank you, they're delicious.

    B. I think you have three.

    C. Are they chocolate?

    * guess〔gɛs〕v. 猜出　　cookie〔'kʊkɪ〕n. 餅乾
    delicious〔dɪ'lɪʃəs〕adj. 美味的
    think〔θɪŋk〕v. 認為（三態變化為：think-thought- thought）
    chocolate〔'tʃɔkəlɪt〕adj. 巧克力的

20. (**B**) Does your dog bite?

    A. Unfortunately, he's very noisy.

    B. No, he's quite gentle.

    C. No, he's not very smart.

    * bite〔baɪt〕v. 咬（三態變化為：bite-bit-bitten）
    unfortunately〔ʌn'fɔrtʃənɪtlɪ〕adv. 不幸地；遺憾地
    noisy〔'nɔɪzɪ〕adj. 吵鬧的　　quite〔kwaɪt〕adv. 非常
    gentle〔'dʒɛntḷ〕adj. 溫和的
    smart〔smɑrt〕adj. 聰明的

第三部份

21.(**C**) M：Sweeping the floor is a boring task.

W：I'll trade you.

M：What are you doing?

W：I'm taking out the garbage.

M：Uh, no thanks.

Question：What does the man mean?

A. He will not thank the woman for taking out the trash.

B. He will take out the trash while the woman sweeps the floor.

C. He would rather sweep the floor than take out the trash.

* sweep〔swip〕*v.* 掃（三態變化為：sweep-swept-swept）

floor〔flor〕*n.* 地板

boring〔'borɪŋ〕*adj.* 無聊的

task〔tæsk〕*n.* 工作；任務

trade〔tred〕*v.* 與…交換　　***take out*** 把…拿出去

garbage〔'gɑrbɪdʒ〕*n.* 垃圾

uh〔ʌ〕*interj.* 嗯（考慮時發出的聲音）

mean〔min〕*v.* 意思是　　trash〔træʃ〕*n.* 垃圾

while〔hwaɪl〕*conj.* 當…的時候

would rather*…*than ～　寧願…，也不願～

22. (**A**) M : Where can I find a taxi to the airport?

W : There are usually some waiting near the corner.

M : Thanks. I'll look there.

W : Would you like some help with your luggage?

M : No, thanks. I've got it.

Question : What is at the corner?

A. Some taxis.

B. The airport.

C. The man's luggage.

* find〔faɪnd〕v. 找到　airport〔'ɛr͵port〕n. 機場

usually〔'juʒʊəlɪ〕adv. 通常

some〔'sʌm〕pron. 一些（在此指「一些計程車」）

near〔nɪr〕prep. 在…附近

corner〔'kɔrnɚ〕n. 轉角

look〔lʊk〕v. 看（有尋找之意）

help〔hɛlp〕n. 幫助　luggage〔'lʌgɪdʒ〕n. 行李

I've got it. 我已經拿好了。

23. (**C**) M : I'd like to take a shower. Are there any bathrooms
on this floor?

W : Yes, there is one, but it has a bathtub.

M : I'd really rather take a shower.

W : Then you can go up the stairs to the fourth floor.

Question : Where will the man wash?

A. In the bathtub.

B. On the stairs.

C. On the fourth floor.

* shower〔ˈʃaʊɚ〕*n.* 淋浴　　***take a shower*** 淋浴

bathroom〔ˈbæθˌrum〕*n.* 浴室　　floor〔flor〕*n.* 樓層

bathtub〔ˈbæθˌtʌb〕*n.* 浴缸　　***would rather V.*** 寧願~

then〔ðɛn〕*adv.* 那麼　　up〔ʌp〕*adv.* 向上

stair〔stɛr〕*n.* 樓梯　　***go up the stairs*** 上樓

fourth〔forθ〕*adj.* 第四個　　wash〔wɑʃ〕*v.* 洗澡

24. (**C**)　M：We should decorate this room.

W：What did you have in mind?

M：How about hanging those pictures we bought?

W：Okay.

Question：What are they going to do?

A. Go shopping for some decorations.

B. Change to another room.

C. Put some pictures on the wall.

* decorate〔ˈdɛkəˌret〕*v.* 裝飾　　mind〔maɪnd〕*n.* 心

What did you have in mind? 你（心裡）有什麼想法？

How about ~? ~如何？　　hang〔hæŋ〕*v.* 懸掛；吊

picture〔ˈpɪktʃɚ〕*n.* 圖畫

buy〔baɪ〕*v.* 買（三態變化為：buy-bought-bought）

shop for 購買（某物）　　***go shopping for*** 去購買（某物）

decoration〔ˌdɛkəˈreʃən〕*n.* 裝飾品

change to ~ 換成~　　another〔əˈnʌðɚ〕*adj.* 另一個

put〔pʊt〕*v.* 放　　wall〔wɔl〕*n.* 牆壁

25. (**C**) M：You should take better care of your plants.

W：What's wrong with them?

M：They need to be repotted. Look, this pot is too small for the roots.

Question：What should the woman do?

A. Buy smaller plants.

B. Cut down the big plants.

C. Put the plants into bigger pots.

* better〔'bɛtɚ〕*adj.* 更好的

  take better care of~ 給~更好的照顧

  plant〔plænt〕*n.* 植物

  What's wrong with~? ~怎麼了？（ = *What's the matter with~?* ）　need〔nid〕*v.* 需要

  repot〔ri'pɑt〕*v.* 重新裝盆

  look〔luk〕*v.* 看哪；瞧　pot〔pɑt〕*n.* 花盆

  root〔rut〕*n.* 根　　cut〔kʌt〕*v.* 切

  cut down 切下　　into〔'ɪntu〕*prep.* 到~之內

  bigger〔'bɪgɚ〕*adj.* 更大的（ big 的比較級 ）

26. (**A**) M：How often do you feed your dog?

W：Twice a day.

M：Is that enough?

W：Sure. He's lived on that for five years.

Question：What does the woman give her dog?

A. She gives him two meals a day.

B. She gives him five years.

C. She gives him only dog food.

* **How often～?** ～多久一次？   feed〔fid〕v. 餵
twice〔twaɪs〕adv. 兩次   sure〔ʃʊr〕adv. 當然
live on～ 靠～維生   for〔fɔr〕prep. 持續
give〔gɪv〕v. 給   meal〔mil〕n. 一餐
only〔'onlɪ〕adv. 只有   **dog food** 狗食

27. (**A**) M：Do you have either a pen or a pencil?

W：No, but I have a marker.

M：That will do. Thanks.

Question：Which of the statements is true?

A. The woman has neither a pen nor a pencil.

B. The man prefers markers to pens and pencils.

C. The man has a pen and a pencil, but no marker.

* **either…or～** 不是…就是～；…或～
marker〔'mɑrkɚ〕n. 馬克筆
do〔du〕v. 行；可以
That will do. 那就可以了。
which〔hwɪtʃ〕pron. 哪一個
statement〔'stetmənt〕n. 敘述
true〔tru〕adj. 正確的
neither…nor～ 既不…也不～
prefer A to B 比較喜歡 A，比較不喜歡 B；喜歡 A 甚於 B

28. (**C**) M：I didn't know you bought a car!

W：I didn't. This is rented.

M：How much is it?

W：NT$1000 a day.

Question：What is true?

A. The woman bought a car for NT$1000 yesterday.

B. The woman borrowed the car for one day.

C. The woman does not own a car.

* know〔no〕v. 知道

buy〔baɪ〕v. 買（三態變化為：buy-bought-bought）

rent〔rɛnt〕v. 租　　borrow〔'baro〕v. 借（入）

own〔on〕v. 擁有

29. (**B**) M：Do you mind if I change the channel?

W：I guess not. What's on?

M：There's a game on at 7:00 that I want to watch.

Question：What are they doing?

A. Going to a game.

B. Watching TV.

C. Looking at the clock.

* mind〔maɪnd〕v. 介意　　channel〔'tʃænl〕n. 頻道

guess〔gɛs〕v. 認為　　on〔an〕adv.（節目）上演中

What's on? 在播什麼節目？　　game〔gem〕n. 比賽

go to a game 去看比賽

watch〔watʃ〕v. 看（電影、電視）

look at 看著　　clock〔klak〕n. 時鐘

30. (**B**) M: Would you like to go sailing today?

W: I don't think today is a good day for it.

M: Why not? It's perfectly clear.

W: Yes, but there's no wind.

Question: Why doesn't the woman want to go sailing?

A. The boat is clean, but it is not comfortable.

B. The boat will not move without wind.

C. She does not want to get wet.

* *Would you like to V. ~ ?* 你想要～嗎？

sail〔sel〕v. 航行

I don't think today is a good day for it. 我不認為
  今天適合航行。

Why not? 為什麼不適合？

perfectly〔'pɝfɪktlɪ〕adv. 完全地；非常

clear〔klɪr〕adj. 晴朗的；乾淨的

wind〔wɪnd〕n. 風　　boat〔bot〕n. 船

comfortable〔'kʌmfətəbl̩〕adj. 舒服的；舒適的

move〔muv〕v. 移動

without〔wɪð'aʊt〕prep. 沒有

get〔gɛt〕v. 變得　　wet〔wɛt〕adj. 濕的

全民英語能力分級檢定測驗
初級測驗⑧

　　本測驗分三部份，全為三選一之選擇題，每部份各 10 題，共 30 題，作答時間約 20 分鐘。

第一部份：看圖辨義
　　　　　本部份共 10 題，試題冊上每題有一個圖片，請聽錄音機播出一個相關的問題，與 A、B、C 三個英語敘述後，選一個與所看到圖片最相符的答案，並在答案紙上相對的圓圈內塗黑作答。每題播出一遍，問題及選項均不印在試題冊上。

例：（看）

NT$80　　NT$50

（聽）

Look at the picture.　How much is the hamburger?

A. It's eighty dollars.
B. It's fifty-five dollars.
C. It's eighteen dollars.

正確答案為 A

Question 1

Question 2

Question 3

Question 4

Question 5

請 翻 頁 ▯▯▯⟹

Question 6

Question 7

Question 8

Question 9

Question 10

請翻頁

第二部份： 問答

　　　　　本部份共 10 題，每題錄音機會播出一個問句或直述句，每題播出一次，聽後請從試題冊上 A、B、C 三個選項中，選出一個最適合的回答或回應，並在答案紙上塗黑作答。

例：

（聽）　Good morning, Kevin. How are you?

（看）　A.　I'm fine, thank you.
　　　　B.　I'm in the living room.
　　　　C.　My name is Kevin.

正確答案爲 A

11. A. It's a picture of my favorite singer.
　　B. That's where we keep the extra chairs.
　　C. The lamp is on the desk.

12. A. No, it's not real.
　　B. Yes. It's my winter coat.
　　C. No. It's not formal enough.

13. A. I always go with the guys.
　　B. Twice a week.
　　C. I like to play basketball.

14. A. No, but my mother is a good cook.
　　B. Yes, I'm still full.
　　C. No, I'm not scared to try it.

15. A. I always have two
       bowls of rice.
    B. No. We ate there last
       week.
    C. No, thanks. I don't
       bowl.

16. A. Yes. I saw it on the
       bulletin board.
    B. No, I didn't know that.
    C. No. I haven't seen her
       today.

17. A. No, I don't have to join
       the military.
    B. Yes, I know who I'm
       going to vote for.
    C. I'm considering
       engineering.

18. A. Yes. I have a glass
       of milk every night.
    B. Yes. I like to paint.
    C. I did, but it ran
       away last week.

19. A. It arrived yesterday.
    B. I just took it to the
       post office.
    C. The mailman
       brought it.

20. A. Poor George!
    B. Is Sam OK?
    C. I'm sure Sam didn't
       mean to hurt him.

請 翻 頁 ⟹

第三部份：簡短對話

本部份共 10 題，每題錄音機會播出一段對話及一個相關的問題，每題播出兩次，聽後請從試題冊上 A、B、C 三個選項中，選出一個最適合的回答，並在答案紙上塗黑作答。

例：

（聽）(Woman) Good afternoon, ...Mr. Davis?

(Man) Yes. I have an appointment with Dr. Sanders at two o'clock. My son Tommy has a fever.

(Woman) Oh, that's too bad. Well, please have a seat, Mr. Davis. Dr. Sanders will be right with you.

Question: Where did this conversation take place?

（看）A. In a post office.

B. In a restaurant.

C. In a doctor's office.

正確答案為 C

21. A. He rules the country.

B. He is really the president.

C. He helps poor people.

22. A. Send a postcard to Ken.

B. Take a picture for Ken.

C. Write an e-mail to Ken.

23. A. They have walked together for two kilometers.
    B. They will walk four kilometers.
    C. They will walk only halfway together.

24. A. It is repaired.
    B. A leg is missing.
    C. It is unstable.

25. A. He is very tall.
    B. He scares the other players.
    C. He is very skillful.

26. A. He is fat.
    B. He should lose a little weight.
    C. He is heavier than his brother.

27. A. It is too cold.
    B. Night is falling.
    C. They might get dirty.

28. A. He is surprised.
    B. He is a basketball player.
    C. He is playing tennis.

29. A. They are worried.
    B. They are angry.
    C. They don't like to talk with her.

30. A. The woman forgot where she keeps it.
    B. He should keep his own diary.
    C. The woman doesn't want to share it.

請 翻 頁 ▌⟹

初級英語聽力檢定⑧詳解

第一部份

Look at the picture for question 1.

1. (**A**)　How is the water?

A. It is warm.

B. It is spring.

C. He is hot.

* water〔'wɔtɚ〕 *n.* 水　　warm〔wɔrm〕*adj.* 溫暖的
spring〔sprɪŋ〕*n.* 泉水　　hot〔hɑt〕*adj.* 熱的

Look at the picture for question 2.

2. (**C**)　Who is studying?

A. English.

B. Sleeping.

C. No one.

* study〔'stʌdɪ〕*v.* 學習　　sleeping〔'slipɪŋ〕*n.* 睡眠

Look at the picture for question 3.

3. (**C**)　What is the man doing?

A. Cooking.

B. Into the cup.

C. Making tea.

* cook〔kʊk〕*v.* 烹飪　　into〔'ɪntu〕*prep.* 到～之內
cup〔kʌp〕*n.* 杯子　　*make tea* 泡茶

Look at the picture for question 4.

4. (**A**) What is she looking at?

    A. The clouds.

    B. It is raining.

    C. Her umbrella.

    * *look at* ~　看著～　　cloud〔klaʊd〕*n.* 雲
    rain〔ren〕*v.* 下雨　　umbrella〔ʌmˈbrɛlə〕*n.* 雨傘

Look at the picture for question 5.

5. (**B**) What does he want to buy?

    A. A piece of paper.

    B. Medicine.

    C. It's a drugstore.

    * piece〔pis〕*n.* 一張　　paper〔ˈpepɚ〕*n.* 紙
    medicine〔ˈmɛdəsṇ〕*n.* 藥
    drugstore〔ˈdrʌɡˌstor〕*n.* 藥房

Look at the picture for question 6.

6. (**C**) What is happening?

    A. The window is breaking.

    B. The boy was playing baseball.

    C. She is punishing him.

    * happen〔ˈhæpən〕*v.* 發生　　window〔ˈwɪndo〕*n.* 窗戶
    break〔brek〕*v.* 破碎；破裂　　play〔ple〕*v.* 打（球）
    baseball〔ˈbesˌbɔl〕*n.* 棒球
    punish〔ˈpʌnɪʃ〕*v.* 處罰

Look at the picture for question 7.

7. (**A**) What did she do?

    A. She washed his face.

    B. She wants to sleep.

    C. She is drying herself.

    * wash〔wɑʃ〕v. 洗　　face〔fes〕n. 臉
      want〔wɑnt〕v. 想要　　sleep〔slip〕v. 睡覺
      dry〔draɪ〕v. 擦乾　　herself〔hɝˋsɛlf〕pron. 她自己

Look at the picture for question 8.

8. (**B**) What happened?

    A. The man has a stomachache.

    B. Something funny happened.

    C. He is exercising.

    * stomachache〔ˋstʌmək͵ek〕n. 胃痛
      something〔ˋsʌmθɪŋ〕pron. 某事
      funny〔ˋfʌnɪ〕adj. 好笑的　　exercise〔ˋɛksɚ͵saɪz〕v. 運動

Look at the picture for question 9.

9. (**B**) Why is he holding his nose?

    A. His nose is running.

    B. The medicine tastes bad.

    C. He does not want to see the medicine.

    * hold〔hold〕v. 抓住；握著　　nose〔noz〕n. 鼻子
      run〔rʌn〕v.（液體等）流出
      His nose is running. 他在流鼻水。
      taste〔test〕v. 嚐起來　　bad〔bæd〕adj.（味道）不好的

Look at the picture for question 10.

10. (**B**) What does the old man do?
A. He drives a bus.　　B. He is a taxi driver.
C. He is driving.

＊ ***What does*** *sb*. ***do?*** 某人從事什麼工作？
drive〔draɪv〕*v.* 駕駛；開車　　bus〔bʌs〕*n.* 公車
taxi〔'tæksɪ〕*n.* 計程車（＝ *cab*）
driver〔'draɪvɚ〕*n.* 駕駛人

第二部份

11. (**A**) What's that on the wall?
A. It's a picture of my favorite singer.
B. That's where we keep the extra chairs.
C. The lamp is on the desk.

＊ wall〔wɔl〕*n.* 牆壁　　picture〔'pɪktʃɚ〕*n.* 相片；圖畫
favorite〔'fevərɪt〕*adj.* 最喜愛的　　singer〔'sɪŋɚ〕*n.* 歌手
where〔hwɛr〕*adv.*（關係副詞）做…的地方
keep〔kip〕*v.* 保存　　extra〔'ɛkstrə〕*adj.* 額外的
chair〔tʃɛr〕*n.* 椅子　　lamp〔læmp〕*n.* 燈

12. (**B**) Is that a warm coat?
A. No, it's not real.　　B. Yes. It's my winter coat.
C. No. It's not formal enough.

＊ warm〔wɔrm〕*adj.* 保暖的　　coat〔kot〕*n.* 外套
real〔'riəl〕*adj.* 真的　　winter〔'wɪntɚ〕*n.* 冬天
formal〔'fɔrml̩〕*adj.* 正式的
enough〔ə'nʌf〕*adv.* 足夠地

13. (**B**) How often do you go to the gym?

    A. I always go with the guys.

    B. Twice a week.

    C. I like to play basketball.

    * ***How often~?*** ～多久一次？
      gym〔dʒɪm〕*n.* 健身房　　always〔'ɔlwez〕*adv.* 總是
      guy〔gaɪ〕*n.*（男）人　　***the guys*** 大夥們（不分男女）
      twice〔twaɪs〕*adv.* 兩次　　week〔wik〕*n.* 星期
      like〔laɪk〕*v.* 喜歡　　basketball〔'bæskɪt,bɔl〕*n.* 籃球

14. (**A**) Are you skillful at cooking?

    A. No, but my mother is a good cook.

    B. Yes, I'm still full.

    C. No, I'm not scared to try it.

    * skillful〔'skɪlfəl〕*adj.* 熟練的
      cooking〔'kʊkɪŋ〕*n.* 烹飪　　cook〔kʊk〕*n.* 廚師
      My mother is a good cook. 我媽媽很會做菜。
      still〔stɪl〕*adv.* 仍然　　full〔fʊl〕*adj.* 飽的
      scared〔skɛrd〕*adj.* 害怕的　　try〔traɪ〕*v.* 嘗試

15. (**C**) Do you want to go bowling after dinner?

    A. I always have two bowls of rice.

    B. No. We ate there last week.

    C. No, thanks. I don't bowl.

    * bowl〔bol〕*v.* 打保齡球　*n.* 碗
      after〔'æftɚ〕*prep.* 在…之後　　dinner〔'dɪnɚ〕*n.* 晚餐
      have〔hæv〕*v.* 吃　　rice〔raɪs〕*n.* 米飯
      there〔ðɛr〕*adv.* 在那裡　　***last week*** 上個星期

16. (**C**) Did you notice Kate's new glasses?

  A. Yes. I saw it on the bulletin board.

  B. No, I didn't know that.

  C. No. I haven't seen her today.

  * notice〔'notɪs〕v. 注意到 glasses〔'glæsɪz〕n. pl. 眼鏡
  see〔si〕v. 看見（三態變化為：see-saw-seen）
  bulletin〔'bulətn̩〕n. 告示 board〔bord〕n. 板
  bulletin board 佈告欄

17. (**C**) Have you picked a major yet?

  A. No, I don't have to join the military.

  B. Yes, I know who I'm going to vote for.

  C. I'm considering engineering.

  * pick〔pɪk〕v. 挑選 major〔'medʒɚ〕n. 主修科目
  yet〔jɛt〕adv. 已經（用於疑問句） ***have to*** 必須
  join〔dʒɔɪn〕v. 加入 military〔'mɪlə,tɛrɪ〕n. 軍隊
  vote〔vot〕v. 投票 ***vote for*** … 投票給…
  consider〔kən'sɪdɚ〕v. 考慮
  engineering〔,ɛndʒə'nɪrɪŋ〕n. 工程學

18. (**B**) Do you have any hobbies?

  A. Yes. I have a glass of milk every night.

  B. Yes. I like to paint.

  C. I did, but it ran away last week.

  * hobby〔'hɑbɪ〕n. 嗜好 ***a glass of*** ~ 一杯~
  milk〔mɪlk〕n. 牛奶 paint〔pent〕v. 畫畫
  run〔rʌn〕v. 跑（三態變化為：run-ran-run）
  run away 逃跑

19. (**A**) When did you receive the package?

    A. It arrived yesterday.

    B. I just took it to the post office.

    C. The mailman brought it.

* receive〔rɪˈsiv〕v. 接到；收到

    package〔ˈpækɪdʒ〕n. 包裹

    arrive〔əˈraɪv〕v. 抵達

    just〔dʒʌst〕adv. 才；剛剛

    take〔tek〕v. 拿   *post office* 郵局

    mailman〔ˈmelˌmæn〕n. 郵差

    bring〔brɪŋ〕v. 帶來（三態變化為：bring-brought-brought）

20. (**A**) Sam said George fell down and hurt himself.

    A. Poor George!

    B. Is Sam OK?

    C. I'm sure Sam didn't mean to hurt him.

* fall〔fɔl〕v. 倒下（三態變化為：fall-fell-fallen）

    fall down 跌倒

    hurt〔hɝt〕v. 傷害；使受傷

    poor〔pur〕adj. 可憐的

    OK〔ˈoˈke〕adj. 好的；沒問題的（= *okay*）

    sure〔ʃur〕adj. 確定的

    mean〔min〕v. 有意

第三部份

21. (**C**)　M：Is there a royal family in your country?

W：Yes, but they no longer have power.

M：What do they do?

W：They mostly do charity work.　The president has
　　the real power.

Question：What does the king of the woman's country
　　　　　do?

A.　He rules the country.

B.　He is really the president.

C.　He helps poor people.

* royal〔'rɔɪəl〕*adj.* 王室的；皇家的

　family〔'fæməlɪ〕*n.* 家庭　　***royal family*** 王室

　country〔'kʌntrɪ〕*n.* 國家

　no longer 不再　　power〔'pauɚ〕*n.* 權力

　What does** sb.* ***do? 某人從事什麼工作?

　mostly〔'mostlɪ〕*adv.* 主要；大多

　charity〔'tʃærətɪ〕*n.* 慈善

　president〔'prɛzədənt〕*n.* 總統

　real〔'riəl〕*adj.* 真正的

　king〔kɪŋ〕*n.* 國王　　rule〔rul〕*v.* 統治

　really〔'riəlɪ〕*adv.* 真正地

　help〔hɛlp〕*v.* 幫助

　poor〔pur〕*adj.* 窮的

22. (**A**) M: Should I send Ken a postcard or an e-mail?

W: An e-mail would be faster.

M: But these pictures are very nice.

W: If he likes pictures, then you should send him one of those.

Question: What will the man probably do?

A. Send a postcard to Ken.

B. Take a picture for Ken.

C. Write an e-mail to Ken.

* should〔ʃʊd〕*aux.* 應該　　send〔sɛnd〕*v.* 寄給

postcard〔'post͵kɑrd〕*n.* 明信片

e-mail〔'i͵mel〕*n.* 電子郵件（electronic mail 的縮寫）

would〔wʊd〕*aux.* will 的過去式

faster〔'fæstə〕*adj.* 較快的（fast 的比較級）

nice〔naɪs〕*adj.* 好的

then〔ðɛn〕*adv.* 那麼

those〔ðoz〕*pron.* 那些（物）

probably〔'prɑbəblɪ〕*adv.* 可能

take a picture 拍照　　write〔raɪt〕*v.* 寫

23. (**B**) M: How far have we walked?

W: About two kilometers.

M: You mean we're only halfway there?

W: Yes. Two more to go.

Question: How far will they walk altogether?

A. They have walked together for two kilometers.

B. They will walk four kilometers.

C. They will walk only halfway together.

* ***How far~?*** ～多遠？　　walk〔wɔk〕v. 走路
  kilometer〔'kɪləˌmitə〕n. 公里　mean〔min〕v. 意思是
  only〔'onlɪ〕adv. 只有
  halfway〔'hæf'we〕adv. 在中途；到一半
  there〔ðɛr〕adv. 往那裡
  Two more to go. 還有兩公里的路要走。
  altogether〔ˌɔltə'gɛðə〕adv. 總共
  together〔tə'gɛðə〕adv. 一起

24.(**C**)　M: This chair should be repaired.

W: What's wrong with it?

M: One of the legs is loose.

W: I'll have it taken care of tomorrow.

Question: What is wrong with the chair?

A. It is repaired.　　B. A leg is missing.

C. It is unstable.

* repair〔rɪ'pɛr〕v. 修理
  What's wrong with~? ～怎麼了；～哪裡不對勁？
  leg〔lɛg〕n. 腳　　loose〔lus〕adj. 鬆動的
  have + sth. + p.p. 使某物被～
  take care of 處理
  I'll have it taken care of tomorrow. 我明天會叫人處理。
  missing〔'mɪsɪŋ〕adj. 失蹤的；找不到的
  unstable〔ʌn'stebl̩〕adj. 不穩固的

25. (**A**) M: Ethan is really good at basketball.

W: He should be. He's a giant compared to the other players.

M: Yes, but he's also very skillful.

Question: What does the woman say about Ethan?

A. He is very tall.

B. He scares the other players.

C. He is very skillful.

* ***be good at*** 擅長　　basketball〔'bæskɪt,bɔl〕*n.* 籃球

giant〔'dʒaɪənt〕*n.* 巨人　　compare〔kəm'pɛr〕*v.* 比較

compare to… 和…比起來　　player〔'pleɚ〕*n.* 球員

also〔'ɔlso〕*adv.* 也

skillful〔'skɪlfəl〕*adj.* 有技巧的；熟練的

scare〔skɛr〕*v.* 使害怕；驚嚇

26. (**B**) M: My brother is on a diet.

W: But he's not overweight, is he?

M: He's a little chubby.

Question: What does the man say about his brother?

A. He is fat.

B. He should lose a little weight.

C. He is heavier than his brother.

* ***on a diet*** 節食　　overweight〔'ovɚ'wet〕*adj.* 過重的

chubby〔'tʃʌbɪ〕*adj.* 圓胖的　　fat〔fæt〕*adj.* 胖的

lose〔luz〕*v.* 減少　　weight〔wet〕*n.* 體重

lose weight 減肥

heavier〔'hɛvɪɚ〕*adj.* 較重的（heavy 的比較級）

27. (**B**) M：Are the children playing in the yard?

W：Yes, they are.

M：I'll call them inside. It's getting dark.

Question：Why must the children come inside?

A. It is too cold.　　B. Night is falling.

C. They might get dirty.

* children〔'tʃɪldrən〕*n. pl.* 小孩（child 的複數）
play〔ple〕*v.* 玩　　yard〔jɑrd〕*n.* 院子
call〔kɔl〕*v.* 叫喚　　inside〔'ɪn'saɪd〕*adv.* 向室內
be getting～ 越來越～　　dark〔dɑrk〕*adj.* 暗的
must〔mʌst〕*aux.* 必須　　cold〔kold〕*adj.* 寒冷的
fall〔fɔl〕*v.* 降臨；到來　　might〔maɪt〕*aux.* 可能
get〔gɛt〕*v.* 變得　　dirty〔'dɜtɪ〕*adj.* 髒的

28. (**C**) M：Is Ted on the basketball court as usual?

W：No. He's on the tennis court.

M：That's a surprise.

Question：What is Ted doing?

A. He is surprised.

B. He is a basketball player.

C. He is playing tennis.

* court〔kort〕*n.* 球場
usual〔'juʒʊəl〕*adj.* 通常的；平常的
as usual 像往常一樣　　tennis〔'tɛnɪs〕*n.* 網球
surprise〔sə'praɪz〕*n.* 令人驚訝的事
surprised〔sə'praɪzd〕*adj.* 驚訝的
player〔'pleə〕*n.* 球員

29. (**A**) M: I'm concerned about Gina.

W: Me, too. She's missed three classes this week.

M: If she misses too many classes she might fail.

W: Someone should talk to her.

Question: How do they feel about Gina?

A. They are worried.

B. They are angry.

C. They don't like to talk with her.

* concerned〔kən'sɜnd〕*adj.* 擔心的

be concerned about 擔心　　miss〔mɪs〕*v.* 缺（課）

class〔klæs〕*n.* 課程　　fail〔fel〕*v.* 不及格

feel〔fil〕*v.* 覺得　　worried〔'wɜɪd〕*adj.* 擔心的

angry〔'æŋgrɪ〕*adj.* 生氣的

30. (**C**) M: Do you keep a diary?

W: Yes. I write in it every night.

M: Can I read it?

W: No. It's private.

Question: Why can't the man read the diary?

A. The woman forgot where she keeps it.

B. He should keep his own diary.

C. The woman doesn't want to share it.

* keep〔kip〕*v.* (持續地) 記；保存

diary〔'daɪərɪ〕*n.* 日記　　**keep a diary** 寫日記

private〔'praɪvɪt〕*adj.* 私人的　　forget〔fə'gɛt〕*v.* 忘記

own〔on〕*adj.* 自己的　　share〔ʃɛr〕*v.* 分享

全民英語能力分級檢定測驗

初級測驗⑨

　　本測驗分三部份，全為三選一之選擇題，每部份各 10 題，共 30 題，作答時間約 20 分鐘。

第一部份：看圖辨義

　　　　本部份共 10 題，試題冊上每題有一個圖片，請聽錄音機播出一個相關的問題，與 A、B、C 三個英語敘述後，選一個與所看到圖片最相符的答案，並在答案紙上相對的圓圈內塗黑作答。每題播出一遍，問題及選項均不印在試題冊上。

例：（看）

NT$80　NT$50

（聽）

Look at the picture.　How much is the hamburger?

　　A.　It's eighty dollars.

　　B.　It's fifty-five dollars.

　　C.　It's eighteen dollars.

正確答案為 A

A. Question 1

B. Question 2

Susan

Kate

C. Question 3

D. **Question 4**

E. **Question 5**

請翻頁 ▯▯▯⟹

F. **Question 6**

G. **Question 7**

H. Question 8

I. Questions 9-10

請 翻 頁 ▯⟹

第二部份： 問答

本部份共 10 題，每題錄音機會播出一個問句或直述句，
每題播出一次，聽後請從試題冊上 A、B、C 三個選項
中，選出一個最適合的回答或回應，並在答案紙上塗黑
作答。

例：

（聽） Good morning, Kevin. How are you?

（看） A. I'm fine, thank you.
　　　 B. I'm in the living room.
　　　 C. My name is Kevin.

正確答案為 A

11. A. No, we're not lost.
　　B. I think the tire is
　　　 flat.
　　C. No, it's the right car.

12. A. I live in Taichung.
　　B. There are twelve
　　　 stories.
　　C. The third.

13. A. Here is a tissue.
　　B. Try these pills.
　　C. I can give you NT$50.

14. A. No, I've never met
　　　 him.
　　B. Yes, his vocabulary is
　　　 quite large.
　　C. Yes. I know it well.

15. A. Yes, I love to go to
       the beach.
    B. No. I'm not a very
       good swimmer.
    C. No. I only like to
       swim in the summer.

16. A. No, but I just moved
       here.
    B. Thank you, I'd love to.
    C. How about next
       Saturday?

17. A. I really hope they win.
    B. I like the Dragons.
    C. No. I just play for
       fun.

18. A. Yes. We'll leave as
       soon as it gets dark.
    B. Yes, we have to
       leave it there.
    C. Yes, so set your
       alarm for 5:00 a.m.

19. A. Are you all right?
    B. Just put it on the
       table.
    C. How about Hong
       Kong?

20. A. Yes, it was delicious.
    B. Yes, I saw a whale.
    C. We fed bread to the
       fish.

請 翻 頁 ▐▶

第三部份： 簡短對話

　　本部份共 10 題，每題錄音機會播出一段對話及一個相關的問題，每題播出兩次，聽後請從試題冊上 A、B、C 三個選項中，選出一個最適合的回答，並在答案紙上塗黑作答。

例：

（聽）(Woman)　Good afternoon, …Mr. Davis?

　　　(Man)　　Yes. I have an appointment with Dr. Sanders at two o'clock. My son Tommy has a fever.

　　　(Woman)　Oh, that's too bad. Well, please have a seat, Mr. Davis. Dr. Sanders will be right with you.

　　　Question: Where did this conversation take place?

（看）A. In a post office.
　　　B. In a restaurant.
　　　C. In a doctor's office.

　　　正確答案為 C

21. A. Yes, but she hid it
   behind her back.
   B. No. She put it back.
   C. Yes, and she doesn't
   care who knows it.

22. A. She is confident that
   he will finish the
   work.
   B. She is thankful that
   he will do the work.
   C. She feels uncertain
   that he can finish the
   work.

23. A. Tomorrow afternoon.
   B. At lunchtime.
   C. Tomorrow morning.

24. A. He bought it.
   B. He borrowed it.
   C. It was a gift.

25. A. It's not really hers.
   B. It's not real.
   C. It's not cheap.

26. A. He lost it.
   B. He threw it away.
   C. He returned it.

27. A. She feels clumsy.
   B. She is in terrible pain.
   C. She is in a little pain.

28. A. She calls him regularly.
   B. She visits him often.
   C. They write letters to
   each other.

29. A. Open the windows
   before the bird gets
   away.
   B. Catch the bird.
   C. Get the bird out of the
   house.

30. A. A jar of spaghetti sauce.
   B. A key for the kitchen
   door.
   C. A package of spaghetti.

請 翻 頁

初級英語聽力檢定⑨詳解

第一部份

For question number 1, please look at picture A.

1. (**B**) Where is the woman sitting?

       A. In the line.   B. Behind the cash register.

       C. It's a basket.

       * sit〔sɪt〕v. 坐   line〔laɪn〕n.（等待順序的）行列
         in the line 在隊伍中   behind〔bɪ'haɪnd〕prep. 在…後面
         cash〔kæʃ〕n. 現金   register〔'rɛdʒɪstɚ〕n. 自動記錄器
         cash register 收銀機   basket〔'bæskɪt〕n. 籃子

For question number 2, please look at picture B.

2. (**A**) What is Susan playing?

       A. The piano.   B. With Kate.

       C. On a chair.

       * play〔ple〕v. 彈；演奏   piano〔pɪ'æno〕n. 鋼琴
         with〔wɪθ〕prep. 和…一起   chair〔tʃɛr〕n. 椅子

For question number 3, please look at picture C.

3. (**C**) Is there a napkin on the table?

       A. No. No one is there.

       B. Yes, it's under the table.

       C. Yes, there is.

       * napkin〔'næpkɪn〕n. 餐巾   table〔'tebl〕n. 桌子
         there〔ðɛr〕adv. 在那裡   under〔'ʌndɚ〕prep. 在…之下

For question number 4, please look at picture D.

4. (**B**) Who is mountain climbing?

     A. Yes, he is.

     B. A boy.

     C. A rope.

     * mountain〔'mauntn̩〕*n.* 山

       climb〔klaɪm〕*v.* 攀爬　　rope〔rop〕*n.* 繩子

For question number 5, please look at picture E.

5. (**A**) What does the woman have?

     A. A pot of coffee.

     B. Would you like some more?

     C. No, he doesn't.

     * pot〔pɑt〕*n.* 壺　　coffee〔'kɔfɪ〕*n.* 咖啡

     Would you like some more? 你想再來一點嗎？

For question number 6, please look at picture F.

6. (**C**) Are there any curtains in the room?

     A. Yes. They are on the bed.

     B. No, there aren't.

     C. Yes. They are on the window.

     * curtain〔'kɝtn̩〕*n.* 窗簾　　bed〔bɛd〕*n.* 床

     window〔'wɪndo〕*n.* 窗戶

For question number 7, please look at picture G.

7. (**C**) How much does it weigh?

    A. Yes, it weighs a lot.

    B. It was weighed on the scale.

    C. It weighs 20 kg.

    * weigh〔we〕v. 重…；稱重

      weigh a lot 很重   scale〔skel〕n. 磅秤

      kg 公斤（= kilogram〔ˈkɪləˌgræm〕）

For question number 8, please look at picture H.

8. (**B**) Why is the girl there?

    A. She likes to read.

    B. She is washing some clothes.

    C. She is a cook.

    * there〔ðɛr〕adv. 在那裡   like〔laɪk〕v. 喜歡

      read〔rid〕v. 讀書   wash〔wɑʃ〕v. 洗

      clothes〔kloðz〕n. pl. 衣服   cook〔kʊk〕n. 廚師

For questions number 9 and 10, please look at picture I.

9. (**B**) Who is Eric?

    A. He is watching.   B. He is the lifeguard.

    C. He is a surfer.

    * watch〔wɑtʃ〕v. 監視；看守

      lifeguard〔ˈlaɪfˌgɑrd〕n. 救生員

      surfer〔ˈsɝfɚ〕n. 衝浪者

10. (**B**) Please look at picture I again. How many people are
in the rowboat?
A. One — Sean.
B. One — David.
C. Three — David, Sean and Tony.

* rowboat〔'ro͵bot〕*n.*（用槳划的）船

第二部份

11. (**B**) What's wrong with the car?
A. No, we're not lost.
B. I think the tire is flat.
C. No, it's the right car.

* ***What's wrong with～?*** ～怎麼了；～哪裡不對勁？
lost〔lɔst〕*adj.* 迷路的
think〔θɪŋk〕*v.* 認爲（三態變化爲：think-thought-thought）
tire〔taɪr〕*n.* 輪胎   flat〔flæt〕*adj.*（輪胎）沒氣的
right〔raɪt〕*adj.* 對的；正確的

12. (**C**) Which floor do you live on?
A. I live in Taichung.
B. There are twelve stories.
C. The third.

* which〔hwɪtʃ〕*adj.* 哪一個   floor〔flor〕*n.* 樓層
live〔lɪv〕*v.* 住   Taichung〔'taɪ'tʃuŋ〕*n.* 台中
story〔'storɪ〕*n.* 樓層
third〔θɝd〕*n.* 第三（在此指 the third floor「三樓」）

13. (**B**) Can you give me something for this cough?

    A. Here is a tissue.

    B. Try these pills.

    C. I can give you NT$50.

    * give〔gɪv〕v. 給　　something〔'sʌmθɪŋ〕pron. 某物
      for〔fɔr〕prep. 爲（治療）…　　cough〔kɔf〕n. 咳嗽
      Here is ~. 這是~。　　tissue〔'tɪʃu〕n. 面紙；衛生紙
      try〔traɪ〕v. 嘗試　　these〔ðiz〕adj. 這些
      pill〔pɪl〕n. 藥丸

14. (**C**) Have you mastered the vocabulary that Mr. Brown
        asked us to learn?

    A. No, I've never met him.

    B. Yes, his vocabulary is quite large.

    C. Yes. I know it well.

    * master〔'mæstə〕v. 精通
      vocabulary〔və'kæbjə,lɛrɪ〕n. 字彙
      ask〔æsk〕v. 要求　　learn〔lɜn〕v. 學習
      never〔'nɛvə〕adv. 從未
      meet〔mit〕v. 和…見面；認識（三態變化爲：meet-met-met）
      quite〔kwaɪt〕adv. 非常
      large〔lɑrdʒ〕adj. 多的
      his vocabulary is quite large 他懂得的字彙非常多
      know〔no〕v. 熟悉；精通
      well〔wɛl〕adv. 充分地；全然地
      know ~ well 對~很熟悉

15. (**B**) Do you like to swim in the deep end?

    A. Yes, I love to go to the beach.

    B. No. I'm not a very good swimmer.

    C. No. I only like to swim in the summer.

    * swim〔swɪm〕v. 游泳

      deep〔dip〕adj. 深的　　end〔ɛnd〕n. 一端

      love〔lʌv〕v. 很喜歡　　beach〔bitʃ〕n. 海邊

      swimmer〔'swɪmɚ〕n. 游泳者

      I'm not a very good swimmer. 我不是很會游泳。

      only〔'onlɪ〕adv. 只

      summer〔'sʌmɚ〕n. 夏天

16. (**A**) Are you a visitor here?

    A. No, but I just moved here.

    B. Thank you, I'd love to.

    C. How about next Saturday?

    * visitor〔'vɪzɪtɚ〕n. 觀光客；訪客

      here〔hɪr〕adv. 到這裡

      just〔dʒʌst〕adv. 才；剛剛

      move〔muv〕v. 搬家

      would love to 想要（= *would like to* ）

      How about~? ~如何？

      next〔nɛkst〕adj. 下一個

      Saturday〔'sætɚde, -dɪ〕n. 星期六

17. (**C**) Are you on the team?

　　A. I really hope they win.

　　B. I like the Dragons.

　　C. No. I just play for fun.

　　* team〔tim〕*n.* 隊　　***on the team*** 隊中的成員

　　　hope〔hop〕*v.* 希望

　　　win〔wɪn〕*v.* 贏（三態變化爲：win-won-won）

　　　dragon〔'drægən〕*n.* 龍（Dragons 在此表隊名「龍隊」）

　　　just〔dʒʌst〕*adv.* 只是

　　　play〔ple〕*v.* 打（球）

　　　fun〔fʌn〕*n.* 樂趣　　***play for fun*** 打好玩的

18. (**C**) Do we really have to leave at dawn?

　　A. Yes. We'll leave as soon as it gets dark.

　　B. Yes, we have to leave it there.

　　C. Yes, so set your alarm for 5:00 a.m.

　　* really〔'rɪəlɪ〕*adv.* 眞地　　***have to*** 必須

　　　leave〔liv〕*v.* 離開；遺留

　　　dawn〔dɔn〕*n.* 黎明　　***~as soon as*** … 一…就~

　　　get〔gɛt〕*v.* 變得　　dark〔dɑrk〕*adj.* 暗的

　　　so〔so〕*adv.* 所以　　set〔sɛt〕*v.* 設定

　　　alarm〔ə'lɑrm〕*n.* 鬧鐘

　　　for〔fɔr〕*prep.* 在…時候

　　　a.m.〔'e'ɛm〕*adv.* 早上（= *A.M.*）

19. (**C**) Let's take a trip somewhere.

A. Are you all right?

B. Just put it on the table.

C. How about Hong Kong?

* let〔lɛt〕 *v.* 讓　　***let's + V.*** 讓我們～吧。

trip〔trɪp〕 *n.* 旅行　　***take a trip*** 去旅行

somewhere〔'sʌm͵hwɛr〕 *adv.* 到某處

Are you all right? 你還好吧？

just〔dʒʌst〕 *adv.* 就（委婉的祈使語氣）

put〔pʊt〕 *v.* 放　　table〔'tebḷ〕 *n.* 桌子

How about ～? ～如何；～怎麼樣？

Hong Kong 〔'haŋ'kaŋ〕 *n.* 香港

20. (**A**) Did you have any seafood at the beach?

A. Yes, it was delicious.

B. Yes, I saw a whale.

C. We fed bread to the fish.

* have〔hæv〕 *v.* 吃

seafood〔'si͵fud〕 *n.* 海鮮

beach〔bitʃ〕 *n.* 海邊

delicious〔dɪ'lɪʃəs〕 *adj.* 美味的

see〔si〕 *v.* 看見（三態變化為：see-saw-seen）

whale〔hwel〕 *n.* 鯨魚

feed〔fid〕 *v.* 餵（三態變化為：feed-fed-fed）

bread〔brɛd〕 *n.* 麵包　　fish〔fɪʃ〕 *n.* 魚

第三部份

21. (**A**) M: Meg, you know you're not allowed to eat candy.

W: I'm not.

M: Then what is that concealed behind your back?

Question: Was Meg eating candy?

A. Yes, but she hid it behind her back.

B. No. She put it back.

C. Yes, and she doesn't care who knows it.

* allow〔ə'laʊ〕v. 允許
  candy〔'kændɪ〕n. 糖果　　then〔ðɛn〕adv. 那麼
  conceal〔kən'sil〕v. 隱藏
  behind〔bɪ'haɪnd〕prep. 在…後面
  back〔bæk〕n. 背　adv. 返回
  hide〔haɪd〕v. 隱藏（三態變化為：hide-hid〔hɪd〕-hid）
  put back　（東西）放回原位
  care〔kɛr〕v. 在乎

22. (**C**) M: Who is going to type the final report?

W: Paul said he would do it.

M: Do you think he can finish it by himself?

W: I doubt it.

Question: What does the woman say about Paul?

A. She is confident that he will finish the work.

B. She is thankful that he will do the work.

C. She feels uncertain that he can finish the work.

* type〔taɪp〕v. 打字　　final〔'faɪnḷ〕adj. 最後的

report〔rɪ'port〕n. 報告　　*final report* 期末報告

would〔wʊd〕aux. 會…（will 的過去式）

finish〔'fɪnɪʃ〕v. 完成；做完（在此指「打完」）

himself〔hɪm'sɛlf〕pron. 他自己

by himself（靠）他自己　　doubt〔daʊt〕v. 懷疑

confident〔'kɑnfədənt〕adj. 有信心的

work〔wɝk〕v. 工作

thankful〔'θæŋkfəl〕adj. 感謝的；感激的

uncertain〔ʌn'sɝtn̩〕adj. 不確定的

23.（**C**）M：Could you lend me your history book?

W：I guess so. When will you return it?

M：How about tomorrow afternoon?

W：I'll need it before lunch.

M：Okay.

Question：When will the man return the book?

A. Tomorrow afternoon.　　B. At lunchtime.

C. Tomorrow morning.

* could〔kʊd〕aux. 能　　lend〔lɛnd〕v. 借（出）

history〔'hɪstrɪ〕n. 歷史　　guess〔gɛs〕v. 猜想；認為

so〔so〕adv. 是那樣（承接前句的內容）

I guess so. 我想可以。　　return〔rɪ'tɝn〕v. 歸還

tomorrow〔tə'mɑro〕n. 明天

afternoon〔ˌæftɚ'nun〕n. 下午

need〔nid〕v. 需要　　before〔bɪ'for〕prep. 在…之前

lunch〔lʌntʃ〕n. 午餐　　okay〔'o'ke〕adv. 好（= OK）

lunchtime〔'lʌntʃˌtaɪm〕n. 午餐時間

24. (**A**)　M：I just got a new car.

　　　　W：That's a big purchase.

　　　　M：Yes, but I bought it from my uncle.

　　　　W：Then I guess you got a good price.

　　　Question：How did the man get his car?

　　　A.　He bought it.

　　　B.　He borrowed it.

　　　C.　It was a gift.

　　* get〔gɛt〕v. 買；得到
　　　 purchase〔'pɝtʃəs〕n. 採購
　　　 buy〔baɪ〕v. 買（三態變化為：buy-bought-bought）
　　　 from〔frɑm〕prep. 從…
　　　 uncle〔'ʌŋkl̩〕n. 叔叔　　price〔praɪs〕n. 價格
　　　 borrow〔'bɑro〕v. 借（入）
　　　 gift〔gɪft〕n. 禮物

25. (**B**)　M：Those earrings are beautiful.

　　　　W：Thank you.　I just got them.

　　　　M：They must have been very expensive.

　　　　W：Oh, no.　The diamonds aren't genuine.

　　　Question：What does the woman say about her
　　　　　　　 jewelry?

　　　A.　It's not really hers.

　　　B.　It's not real.

　　　C.　It's not cheap.

* those〔 ðoz 〕 *adj.* 那些　　earrings〔 'ɪr,rɪŋz 〕 *n. pl.* 耳環
beautiful〔 'bjutəfəl 〕 *adj.* 美麗的　　get〔 gɛt 〕 *v.* 買
must〔 mʌst 〕 *aux.* 一定
must have + p.p. 當時一定~（表示對過去的肯定推測）
expensive〔 ɪk'spɛnsɪv 〕 *adj.* 昂貴的
oh〔 o 〕 *interj.* 喔　　***Oh, no.*** 噢，不。
diamond〔 'daɪəmənd 〕 *n.* 鑽石
genuine〔 'dʒɛnjuɪn 〕 *adj.* 眞的；純粹的
jewelry〔 'dʒuəlrɪ 〕 *n.* 珠寶　　really〔 'rɪəlɪ 〕 *adv.* 眞地
hers〔 hɝz 〕 *pron.* 她的（東西）　　real〔 'rɪəl 〕 *adj.* 眞的
cheap〔 tʃip 〕 *adj.* 便宜的

26. (**B**) M：I think I should return this shirt.

W：Why?

M：It's a little too small.

W：Do you still have the receipt?

M：No, but I'll look for it in the wastebasket.

Question：What did the man do with the receipt?

A. He lost it.　　　　B. He threw it away.

C. He returned it.

* should〔 ʃud 〕 *aux.* 應該　　return〔 rɪ'tɝn 〕 *v.* 退回
shirt〔 ʃɝt 〕 *n.* 襯衫　　***a little*** 有點；稍微
still〔 stɪl 〕 *adv.* 仍然　　receipt〔 rɪ'sit 〕 *n.* 收據
look for 尋找　　wastebasket〔 'west,bæskɪt 〕 *n.* 廢紙簍
do with 處理
lose〔 luz 〕 *v.* 遺失（三態變化爲：lose-lost-lost）
throw〔 θro 〕 *v.* 丟（三態變化爲：throw-threw〔 θru 〕-thrown）
throw away 丟掉

27. (**C**)　M：What a shame that you broke your leg!

W：Yes, it was clumsy of me.

M：Is it very painful?

W：It was at first, but now the pain is tolerable.

Question：How does the woman feel now?

A. She feels clumsy.

B. She is in terrible pain.

C. She is in a little pain.

* shame〔ʃek〕 *n.* 遺憾的事；可惜的事

    What a shame! 眞可憐；眞倒楣！

    break〔brek〕 *v.* 折斷（三態變化爲：break-broke-broken）

    leg〔lɛg〕 *n.* 腳　　clumsy〔'klʌmzɪ〕 *adj.* 笨拙的

    painful〔'penfəl〕 *adj.* 疼痛的

    at first 起初；一開始　　pain〔pen〕 *n.* 疼痛

    tolerable〔'talərəb!〕 *adj.* 可忍受的

    feel〔fil〕 *v.* 覺得　　terrible〔'tɛrəb!〕 *adj.* 劇烈的

    a little 有點；稍微　　***be in a little pain*** 有點痛

28. (**C**)　M：I haven't seen Max since he moved overseas.

W：Neither have I, but we correspond regularly.

M：That's a good way to keep in touch.

Question：How does the woman keep in touch
　　　　　with Max?

A. She calls him regularly.

B. She visits him often.

C. They write letters to each other.

* since〔sɪns〕*conj.* 自從　　move〔muv〕*v.* 搬家

overseas〔'ovɚ'siz〕*adv.* 到海外

neither〔'niðɚ〕*adv.* 也不

correspond〔,kɔrə'spɑnd〕*v.* 通信

regularly〔'rɛgjələlɪ〕*adv.* 定期地

way〔we〕*n.* 方法　　keep〔kip〕*v.* 保持

touch〔tʌtʃ〕*n.* 連繫　　***keep in touch*** 保持連絡

call〔kɔl〕*v.* 打電話給～　　visit〔'vɪzɪt〕*v.* 拜訪

often〔'ɔfən〕*adv.* 經常　　write〔raɪt〕*v.* 寫

letter〔'lɛtɚ〕*n.* 信　　***each other*** 彼此；互相

29. (**B**)　M：Oh, no! The bird got out of its cage.

W：Where is it?

M：I guess it's somewhere in the house.

W：Then we'd better capture it before we open any windows.

Question：What will they try to do?

A. Open the windows before the bird gets away.

B. Catch the bird.

C. Get the bird out of the house.

* ***Oh, no!*** 噢，糟了！　　***get out of*** … 由…出去（來）

cage〔kedʒ〕*n.* 籠子　　guess〔gɛs〕*v.* 猜想

had better + *V.* 最好～　　capture〔'kæptʃɚ〕*v.* 捕捉

before〔bɪ'for〕*prep.* 在…之前

open〔'opən〕*v.* 打開

try〔traɪ〕*v.* 嘗試　　***get away*** 離開

catch〔kætʃ〕*v.* 捕捉　　***get ～ out of*** … 使～離開…

30. (**C**) M：Let's make some spaghetti.

W：Okay, but we'll have to go to the store first.

M：I just bought a jar of spaghetti sauce.

W：Yes, but we're missing the key ingredient — the pasta!

Question：What will they buy at the store?

A. A jar of spaghetti sauce.

B. A key for the kitchen door.

C. A package of spaghetti.

* make〔mek〕*v.* 做

spaghetti〔spə'gɛtɪ〕*n.* 義大利麵

store〔stor〕*n.* 商店   first〔fɝst〕*adv.* 先

just〔dʒʌst〕*adv.* 才；剛剛

jar〔dʒɑr〕*n.* 一瓶   *a jar of* ~ 一瓶~

sauce〔sɔs〕*n.* 醬汁；調味醬

miss〔mɪs〕*v.* 遺漏

key〔ki〕*adj.* 重要的   *n.* 鑰匙

ingredient〔ɪn'gridɪənt〕*n.* 原料

pasta〔'pɑstə〕*n.* 通心粉；義大利麵

package〔'pækɪdʒ〕*n.* 包   *a package of* ~ 一包~

全民英語能力分級檢定測驗
初級測驗⑩

　　本測驗分三部份，全為三選一之選擇題，每部份各 10 題，共 30 題，作答時間約 20 分鐘。

第一部份：看圖辨義
　　　　　本部份共 10 題，試題冊上每題有一個圖片，請聽錄音機播出一個相關的問題，與 A、B、C 三個英語敘述後，選一個與所看到圖片最相符的答案，並在答案紙上相對的圈圈內塗黑作答。每題播出一遍，問題及選項均不印在試題冊上。

例：（看）

NT$80　NT$50

（聽）

Look at the picture.　How much is the hamburger?

　　A.　It's eighty dollars.
　　B.　It's fifty-five dollars.
　　C.　It's eighteen dollars.

正確答案為 A

A. **Question 1**

B. **Question 2**

C. <u>Question 3</u>

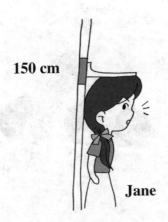

D. <u>Questions 4-5</u>

請 翻 頁 ▮◻⟹

E. **Question 6**

F. **Question 7**

G. **Question 8**

H. **Question 9**

I. **Question 10**

請翻頁 ⬛▷

第二部份： 問答

本部份共 10 題，每題錄音機會播出一個問句或直述句，每題播出一次，聽後請從試題冊上 A、B、C 三個選項中，選出一個最適合的回答或回應，並在答案紙上塗黑作答。

例：

（聽）　Good morning, Kevin.　How are you?

（看）　A.　I'm fine, thank you.
　　　　B.　I'm in the living room.
　　　　C.　My name is Kevin.

正確答案為 A

11. A. What did he name it?
　　B. He should return it.
　　C. I hope he gets better soon.

12. A. In case I fall off my motorbike.
　　B. I don't want to breathe the dirty air.
　　C. The sun is very strong today.

13. A. No.　I still live in Taipei.
　　B. Let me look in my wallet.
　　C. No, I don't have any chance.

14. A. That's a big debt.
　　B. However will you pay him back?
　　C. You should call the police!

15. A. It doesn't open until 9:00.

    B. I lost the key.

    C. There is no electricity.

16. A. It doesn't speak English.

    B. It says, "hiss hiss."

    C. It says I weigh 70 kilos.

17. A. Yes, I have enough time
      to watch it.

    B. It's in the living room.

    C. What channel is it on?

18. A. There is a garage across
      the street.

    B. I like to play in Green
      Park.

    C. Yes, you can.

19. A. No, we needn't.

    B. Yes, we have to
      wear them.

    C. Yes, every room
      looks different.

20. A. Sorry. I'll refill it
      right away.

    B. All the students
      are outside.

    C. The lions were
      moved to another
      one.

請 翻 頁 ▌⟹

第三部份： 簡短對話

本部份共 10 題，每題錄音機會播出一段對話及一個相關的問題，每題播出兩次，聽後請從試題冊上 A、B、C 三個選項中，選出一個最適合的回答，並在答案紙上塗黑作答。

例：

（聽）(Woman)　Good afternoon, ...Mr. Davis?

　　　(Man)　　Yes.　I have an appointment with Dr. Sanders at two o'clock.　My son Tommy has a fever.

　　　(Woman)　Oh, that's too bad.　Well, please have a seat, Mr. Davis.　Dr. Sanders will be right with you.

　　　Question: Where did this conversation take place?

（看）A.　In a post office.

　　　B.　In a restaurant.

　　　C.　In a doctor's office.

正確答案爲 C

21. A. He will look at the woman's car.

B. He will punish the woman for being late again.

C. He will forget about the woman's lateness.

22. A. The members of the other team were big and strong.

B. She argued with the other team and became upset.

C. The other team had better reasons.

23. A. She told Angela about the secret party.

B. She almost told Angela about the party.

C. She made Angela promise to keep the party a secret.

24. A. They will have a formal meal.

B. They will give the team members prizes.

C. They will shake their hands.

請 翻 頁 ⮞

25. A. She usually loses
     tennis competitions.
   B. She wishes she could
     make more money
     by playing tennis.
   C. She is not a
     professional tennis
     player.

26. A. It is right next door.
   B. The home delivery is
     convenient.
   C. It takes five days to
     buy the books.

27. A. It was an ordinary
     meal.
   B. It was an unusual
     meal.
   C. It was not what she
     ordered.

28. A. Make the practices
     more fun.
   B. Practice volleyball at
     the beach.
   C. Go on a trip instead
     of practicing
     volleyball.

29. A. Find a way to move
     the chair.
   B. Light up the dark
     corner.
   C. Get rid of the chair.

30. A. Nancy will move to
     Australia next week.
   B. Nancy is complaining
     about having to move.
   C. Nancy is thinking
     about moving.

初級英語聽力檢定 ⑩ 詳解

第一部份

For question number 1, please look at picture A.

1. (**B**) What are they doing?

    A. They are at the beach.

    B. They are having a picnic.

    C. They were swimming.

    * beach〔bitʃ〕*n.* 海邊   picnic〔'pɪknɪk〕*n.* 野餐

    have a picnic 野餐   swim〔swɪm〕*v.* 游泳

For question number 2, please look at picture B.

2. (**A**) Where is the crosswalk?

    A. It is at the intersection.

    B. The boy will cross the street.

    C. She is walking down the street.

    * crosswalk〔'krɔs,wɔlk〕*n.* 行人穿越道

    intersection〔,ɪntə'sɝkʃən〕*n.* 十字路口

    cross〔krɔs〕*v.* 穿越   street〔strit〕*n.* 街道

    walk〔wɔk〕*v.* 走   down〔daʊn〕*prep.* 沿著

For question number 3, please look at picture C.

3. (**B**) What is Jane's height?

    A. It is black.   B. It is 150 centimeters.

    C. She weighs 150 pounds.

    * height〔haɪt〕*n.* 身高；高度   black〔blæk〕*adj.* 黑色的

    centimeter〔'sɛntə,mitə〕*n.* 公分   weigh〔we〕*v.* 重…

    pound〔paʊnd〕*n.* 磅

For questions number 4 and 5, please look at picture D.

4. (**C**) Where can they buy what they want?

    A. They want to buy a handkerchief.

    B. They lost it in the store.

    C. They can buy one on the third floor.

    * what〔hwɑt〕*pron.* …的東西（在此當關係代名詞）

    handkerchief〔'hæŋkɚtʃɪf〕*n.* 手帕

    lose〔luz〕*v.* 遺失（三態變化為：lose-lost-lost）

    store〔stor〕*n.* 商店   third〔θɝd〕*adj.* 第三的

    floor〔flor〕*n.* 樓層

5. (**A**) Please look at picture D again. Who is helping the couple?

    A. He is a clerk.

    B. It is a department store.

    C. They are customers.

    * help〔hɛlp〕*v.* 幫助   couple〔'kʌpl̩〕*n.* 一對男女；夫妻

    clerk〔klɝk〕*n.* 店員   ***department store*** 百貨公司

    customer〔'kʌstəmɚ〕*n.* 顧客

For question number 6, please look at picture E.

6. (**A**) Where is the telescope pointed?

    A. At the stars.   B. A man and his two sons.

    C. Yes, it is.

    * telescope〔'tɛlə,skop〕*n.* 望遠鏡

    point〔pɔɪnt〕*v.* 把…指向；使…朝向

    star〔star〕*n.* 星星   son〔sʌn〕*n.* 兒子

For question number 7, please look at picture F.

7. (**C**) Why is the man running?

    A. He is running fast.

    B. He is celebrating.

    C. He is afraid.

    * run〔rʌn〕*v.* 跑   fast〔fæst〕*adv.* 快速地

    celebrate〔'sɛlə,bret〕*v.* 慶祝

    afraid〔ə'fred〕*adj.* 害怕的

For question number 8, please look at picture G.

8. (**B**) Is the man picking fruit?

    A. Yes, he will pick it up.

    B. No, he is cutting branches.

    C. Yes. It's on the ground.

    * pick〔pɪk〕*v.* 摘   fruit〔frut〕*n.* 水果

    pick up 撿起   cut〔kʌt〕*v.* 剪（三態同形）

    branch〔bræntʃ〕*n.* 樹枝   ground〔graʊnd〕*n.* 地面

For question number 9, please look at picture H.

9. (**A**) Why does the girl want a spoon?

    A. She cannot use chopsticks.

    B. Yes, she wants one.

    C. She likes to eat ice cream.

    * spoon〔spun〕*n.* 湯匙   use〔juz〕*v.* 使用

    chopsticks〔'tʃɑp,stɪks〕*n. pl.* 筷子

    like to V. 想要～；喜歡～   *ice cream* 冰淇淋

For question number 10, please look at picture I.

10. (**B**) What will the boys do?

  A. They will look for a table.

  B. They will join them at the table.

  C. They will invite the girl to lunch.

  * ***look for*** 尋找 join〔dʒɔɪn〕*v.* 加入

   invite〔ɪnˈvaɪt〕*v.* 邀請 lunch〔lʌntʃ〕*n.* 午餐

   invite sb. to lunch 請某人吃午餐

第二部份

11. (**C**) I heard that Alex has a fever.

  A. What did he name it? B. He should return it.

  C. I hope he gets better soon.

  * hear〔hɪr〕*v.* 聽說 fever〔ˈfivɚ〕*n.* 發燒

   have a fever 發燒 name〔nem〕*v.* 替⋯命名

   should〔ʃud〕*aux.* 應該 return〔rɪˈtɜn〕*v.* 歸還

   hope〔hop〕*v.* 希望 get〔gɛt〕*v.* 變得

   get better （病情）好轉 soon〔sun〕*adv.* 馬上；很快地

12. (**B**) Why are you wearing a mask?

  A. In case I fall off my motorbike.

  B. I don't want to breathe the dirty air.

  C. The sun is very strong today.

  * wear〔wɛr〕*v.* 戴；穿 mask〔mæsk〕*n.* 口罩；面具

   in case 以防⋯ ***fall off*** 跌落

   motorbike〔ˈmotɚˌbaɪk〕*n.* 摩托車

   breathe〔brið〕*v.* 呼吸 dirty〔ˈdɜtɪ〕*adj.* 髒的

   air〔ɛr〕*n.* 空氣 sun〔sʌn〕*n.* 太陽；陽光

   strong〔strɔŋ〕*adj.* 強烈的

13. (**B**) Do you have any change?

A. No. I still live in Taipei.

B. Let me look in my wallet.

C. No, I don't have any chance.

* any〔ˋɛnɪ〕*adj.* 任何的　　change〔tʃendʒ〕*n.* 零錢
still〔stɪl〕*adv.* 仍然　　live〔lɪv〕*v.* 住
Taipei〔ˋtaɪˋpe〕*n.* 台北　　let〔lɛt〕*v.* 讓
look〔lʊk〕*v.* 看（有尋找之意）
wallet〔ˋwɑlɪt〕*n.* 皮夾　　chance〔tʃæns〕*n.* 機會

14. (**A**) Mark borrowed NT$20,000 from me.

A. That's a big debt.

B. However will you pay him back?

C. You should call the police!

* borrow〔ˋbɑro〕*v.* 借（入）　　***borrow from ~*** 從~借來
debt〔dɛt〕*n.* 債　　however〔haʊˋɛvɚ〕*adv.* 究竟如何
pay〔pe〕*v.* 付錢　　***pay back*** 還錢
call〔kɔl〕*v.* 打電話給~　　police〔pəˋlis〕*n.* 警方

15. (**B**) Why can't you open your locker?

A. It doesn't open until 9:00.

B. I lost the key.

C. There is no electricity.

* open〔ˋopən〕*v.* 打開　　locker〔ˋlɑkɚ〕*n.* 置物櫃
until〔ənˋtɪl〕*prep.* 直到　　***not…until ~*** 直到~才…
lose〔luz〕*v.* 遺失（三態變化為：lose-lost-lost）
key〔ki〕*n.* 鑰匙　　electricity〔ɪˏlɛkˋtrɪsətɪ〕*n.* 電

16. (**C**) Well, what does the scale say?

A. It doesn't speak English.

B. It says, "hiss hiss."

C. It says I weigh 70 kilos.

* well〔wɛl〕*interj.* 嗯；那麼（用於繼續話題時）
scale〔skel〕*n.* 磅秤　　say〔se〕*v.* 顯示（數字）
speak〔spik〕*v.* 說
hiss〔hɪs〕*n.* 噓（表示制止、不滿、輕蔑等時所發出的聲音）
weigh〔we〕*v.* 重…
kilo〔'kɪlo〕*n.* 公斤（= kilogram〔'kɪlə,græm〕）

17. (**C**) It's nearly time for the TV program to start.

A. Yes, I have enough time to watch it.

B. It's in the living room.

C. What channel is it on?

* nearly〔'nɪrlɪ〕*adv.* 幾乎；將近　　***time for～*** ～的時間
program〔'progræm〕*n.* 節目　　start〔start〕*v.* 開始
enough〔ə'nʌf〕*adj.* 足夠的　　time〔taɪm〕*n.* 時間
watch〔watʃ〕*v.* 看　　***living room*** 客廳
channel〔'tʃænḷ〕*n.* 頻道

18. (**A**) Where can I park?

A. There is a garage across the street.

B. I like to play in Green Park.

C. Yes, you can.

* park〔park〕*v.* 停車　　garage〔gə'raʒ〕*n.* 車庫
across〔ə'krɔs〕*prep.* 在…對面　　street〔strit〕*n.* 街道
green〔grin〕*n.* 綠色　　park〔park〕*n.* 公園

19. (**B**) Does your school require uniforms?

    A. No, we needn't.

    B. Yes, we have to wear them.

    C. Yes, every room looks different.

    * require〔rɪ'kwaɪr〕v. 要求
    uniform〔'junə,fɔrm〕n. 制服
    need〔nɪd〕aux. 需要；有必要（只用於否定句和疑問句）
    have to 必須   wear〔wɛr〕v. 穿
    room〔rum〕n. 室；房間   look〔lʊk〕v. 看起來
    different〔'dɪfərənt〕adj. 不同的

20. (**C**) Why is this cage empty?

    A. Sorry. I'll refill it right away.

    B. All the students are outside.

    C. The lions were moved to another one.

    * cage〔kedʒ〕n. 籠子   empty〔'ɛmptɪ〕adj. 空的
    sorry〔'sɔrɪ〕interj. 對不起   refill〔ri'fɪl〕v. 再注滿
    right away 馬上；立刻   outside〔'aʊt'saɪd〕adv. 在外面
    lion〔'laɪən〕n. 獅子   move〔muv〕v. 遷移
    another〔ə'nʌðə〕adj. 另一個

第三部份

21. (**C**) M：Why are you late?

    W：I had a flat tire on the way to work.

    M：I guess that's not your fault. I'll overlook it this time.

    Question：What will the man do?

    A. He will look at the woman's car.

    B. He will punish the woman for being late again.

    C. He will forget about the woman's lateness.

* late〔let〕adj. 遲到的　　flat〔flæt〕adj.（輪胎）沒氣的
　tire〔taɪr〕n. 輪胎　**have a flat tire** 爆胎
　on the way to… 去…的途中　　work〔wɜk〕n. 工作
　guess〔gɛs〕v. 猜想；認爲　　fault〔fɔlt〕n. 過錯
　overlook〔͵ovɚ'luk〕v. 忽視；不追究　**this time** 這次
　look at 看看　　punish〔'pʌnɪʃ〕v. 處罰
　again〔ə'gɛn〕adv. 再一次　　forget〔fɚ'gɛt〕v. 忘記
　forget about… 對…不放在心上
　lateness〔'letnɪs〕n. 遲到

22. (**C**)　M：How was the debate?

　　　W：We lost.

　　　M：That's too bad.　Are you upset?

　　　W：No.　The other team made stronger arguments.

　　　Question：Why did the woman lose?

　　　A. The members of the other team were big and strong.

　　　B. She argued with the other team and became upset.

　　　C. The other team had better reasons.

* debate〔dɪ'bet〕n. 辯論
　lose〔luz〕v. 輸（三態變化爲：lose-lost-lost）
　That's too bad. 眞可惜。
　upset〔ʌp'sɛt〕adj. 不高興的；心煩的
　the other　（兩者中）另一個　　team〔tim〕n. 隊
　stronger〔'strɔŋgɚ〕adj. 更有說服力的；更強有力的
　　　（strong 的比較級）
　argument〔'ɑrgjəmənt〕n. 論點；理由
　member〔'mɛmbɚ〕n. 成員　　big〔bɪg〕adj. 高大的
　strong〔strɔŋ〕adj. 強壯的　　argue〔'ɑrgju〕v. 爭論
　become〔bɪ'kʌm〕v. 變得
　better〔'bɛtɚ〕adj. 較好的（good 的比較級）
　reason〔'rizn̩〕n. 理由

23. (**B**) M : You didn't tell Angela about the party, did you?

W : No. I was on the verge of doing it when I remembered it was a secret.

Question : What did the woman do?

A. She told Angela about the secret party.

B. She almost told Angela about the party.

C. She made Angela promise to keep the party a secret.

* verge〔vɜdʒ〕*n.* 邊緣　　***on the verge of*** ～　即將～

secret〔'sikrɪt〕*n.* 秘密　*adj.* 秘密的

almost〔'ɔl,most〕*adv.* 幾乎　　promise〔'prɑmɪs〕*v.* 承諾

make *sb.* ***promise to*** ～　要某人承諾～

keep ～ ***a secret***　將～保密

24. (**A**) M : We should congratulate the baseball team.

W : We will. We're holding a banquet to celebrate their championship.

M : That sounds like fun.

Question : How will they congratulate the team?

A. They will have a formal meal.

B. They will give the team members prizes.

C. They will shake their hands.

* congratulate〔kən'grætʃə,let〕*v.* 恭喜

baseball〔'bes,bɔl〕*n.* 棒球　　team〔tim〕*n.* 隊

hold〔hold〕*v.* 舉行　　banquet〔'bæŋkwɪt〕*n.* 宴會

celebrate〔'sɛlə,bret〕*v.* 慶祝

championship〔'tʃæmpɪən,ʃɪp〕*n.* 冠軍

sound like　聽起來像　　formal〔'fɔrml〕*adj.* 正式的

member〔'mɛmbɚ〕*n.* 成員　　prize〔praɪz〕*n.* 獎；獎品

shake *one's* ***hand***　和某人握手

25. (**C**) M：You're a very good tennis player.

W：Thank you.

M：Are you able to make a good living at it?

W：Oh, no. I'm just an amateur.

Question：What does the woman mean?

A. She usually loses tennis competitions.

B. She wishes she could make more money by playing tennis.

C. She is not a professional tennis player.

* tennis（ˋtɛnɪs）n. 網球　　player（ˋpleɚ）n. 球員
  be able to V. 能夠～　　**make a good living** 過優渥的生活
  at（æt）prep. 從事…　　**Oh, no.** 噢，不是的。
  just（dʒʌst）adv. 只是
  amateur（ˋæməˌtʃur）n. 業餘愛好者
  mean（min）v. 意思是　　usually（ˋjuʒuəlɪ）adv. 通常
  lose（luz）v. 輸掉　　competition（ˌkɑmpəˋtɪʃən）n. 比賽
  wish（wɪʃ）v. 希望
  could（kud）aux. 能夠（與現在事實相反的假設用法）
  make（mek）v. 賺（錢）　　more（mor）adj. 更多的
  by（baɪ）prep. 藉由　　play（ple）v. 打（球）
  professional（prəˋfɛʃənḷ）adj. 職業的

26. (**B**) M：I just bought some books online.

W：Is that expensive?

M：Not really, and they'll deliver them right to my door.

W：How long will that take?

M：About five days.

Question：Why does the man like to buy books online?

A. It is right next door.

B. The home delivery is convenient.

C. It takes five days to buy the books.

* just〔dʒʌst〕adv. 才；剛剛
online〔'ɑn,laɪn〕adv. 線上地；在網路上（= on-line）
expensive〔ɪk'spɛnsɪv〕adj. 昂貴的　**not really** 其實不會
deliver〔dɪ'lɪvɚ〕v. 遞送　right〔raɪt〕adv. 直接地；正好
How long ~? ~多久？　take〔tek〕v. 花費（時間）
next door 在隔壁　delivery〔dɪ'lɪvərɪ〕n. 遞送
home delivery 宅配到府
convenient〔kə'vinjənt〕adj. 方便的

27.(**A**) M：Did you enjoy your dinner?

W：It was all right.

M：Just all right?

W：Yeah. The food was pretty average.

Question：How was the woman's meal?

A. It was an ordinary meal.

B. It was an unusual meal.

C. It was not what she ordered.

* enjoy〔ɪn'dʒɔɪ〕v. 喜歡；享受　dinner〔'dɪnɚ〕n. 晚餐
It was all right. 還可以。　just〔dʒʌst〕adv. 只是…而已
yeah〔jæ〕adv. 是的（= yes）　food〔fud〕n. 食物
pretty〔'prɪtɪ〕adv. 非常
average〔'ævərɪdʒ〕adj. 一般的；普通的
meal〔mil〕n. 一餐　ordinary〔'ɔrdn̩,ɛrɪ〕adj. 普通的
unusual〔ʌn'juʒʊəl〕adj. 不尋常的
what〔hwɑt〕pron. …的東西（在此當關係代名詞）
order〔'ɔrdɚ〕v. 點（菜）

28. (**C**)　M：Everyone on the volleyball team feels down after losing the game.

W：How can we cheer them up?

M：Why don't we skip the next practice and just do something fun?

W：That's a good idea.　We could go to the beach.

Question：What will they do to help the team?

A.　Make the practices more fun.

B.　Practice volleyball at the beach.

C.　Go on a trip instead of practicing volleyball.

* volleyball〔'vɑlɪ,bɔl〕n. 排球　　feel〔fil〕v. 覺得

down〔daʊn〕adj. 意志消沈的

game〔gem〕n. 比賽

cheer sb. up　使某人振作；鼓勵某人

skip〔skɪp〕v. 跳過　　next〔nɛkst〕adj. 下一個

practice〔'præktɪs〕n. 練習　v. 練習

just〔dʒʌst〕adv. 就⋯（委婉的祈使語氣）

something〔'sʌmθɪŋ〕pron. 某事

fun〔fʌn〕adj. 好玩的；有趣的

idea〔aɪ'diə〕n. 主意

could〔kʊd〕aux. 可以（can 的未來式）

beach〔bitʃ〕n. 海邊

make〔mek〕v. 使⋯變得～

more〔mor〕adv. 更；更加

trip〔trɪp〕n. 旅行　　*go on a trip*　去旅行

instead of　代替；而不是

29. (**B**) M：You shouldn't read in that corner.　There isn't enough light.

W：But this is the most comfortable chair.

M：Then we'll have to find some way to make it brighter.

Question：What does the man want to do?

A. Find a way to move the chair.

B. Light up the dark corner.

C. Get rid of the chair.

* read〔rɪd〕v. 讀書

corner〔'kɔrnɚ〕n. 角落

enough〔ə'nʌf〕adj. 足夠的

light〔laɪt〕n. 光　v. 照亮（三態變化為：light-lighted-lit）

most〔most〕adj. 最～

comfortable〔'kʌmfɚtəbḷ〕adj. 舒服的

chair〔tʃɛr〕n. 椅子　　　***have to*** 必須

then〔ðɛn〕adv. 那麼

find〔faɪnd〕v. 找　　　some〔sʌm〕adj. 某個

way〔we〕n. 方法

brighter〔'braɪtɚ〕adj. 更亮（bright 的比較級）

move〔muv〕v. 移動　　　***light up*** 照亮

dark〔dɑrk〕adj. 暗的

get rid of 除去；丟棄

30. (**C**) M：Nancy is contemplating moving abroad.

W：Where does she want to go?

M：To Australia. She'll decide by next week.

Question：Which of the following is true?

A. Nancy will move to Australia next week.

B. Nancy is complaining about having to move.

C. Nancy is thinking about moving.

* contemplate〔'kɑntəmˌplet〕*v.* 仔細考慮

move〔muv〕*v.* 搬家

abroad〔ə'brɔd〕*adv.* 到國外

Australia〔ɔ'streljə〕*n.* 澳洲

decide〔dɪ'saɪd〕*v.* 決定

by〔baɪ〕*prep.* 在…以前

next〔nɛkst〕*adj.* 下一個　　week〔wik〕*n.* 星期

which〔hwɪtʃ〕*pron.* 哪一個

following〔'fɑləwɪŋ〕*adj.* 下列的

the following 下列（事物）

true〔tru〕*adj.* 正確的

complain〔kəm'plen〕*v.* 抱怨

complain about ~ 抱怨~　　***think about*** ~ 考慮~

全民英語能力分級檢定測驗
初級測驗⑪

　　本測驗分三部份，全為三選一之選擇題，每部份各 10 題，共 30 題，作答時間約 20 分鐘。

第一部份：看圖辨義

　　　　　本部份共 10 題，試題冊上每題有一個圖片，請聽錄音機播出一個相關的問題，與 A、B、C 三個英語敘述後，選一個與所看到圖片最相符的答案，並在答案紙上相對的圓圈內塗黑作答。每題播出一遍，問題及選項均不印在試題冊上。

例：（看）

NT$80　NT$50

（聽）

Look at the picture.　How much is the hamburger?

A.　It's eighty dollars.
B.　It's fifty-five dollars.
C.　It's eighteen dollars.

正確答案為 A

Question 1

Question 2

Question 3

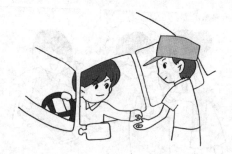

Question 4

Question 5

請翻頁 ▯▯⟹

Question 6

Question 7

Question 8

Question 9

Question 10

請 翻 頁

第二部份： 問答

　　　　本部份共 10 題，每題錄音機會播出一個問句或直述句，
　　　　每題播出一次，聽後請從試題冊上 A、B、C 三個選項
　　　　中，選出一個最適合的回答或回應，並在答案紙上塗黑
　　　　作答。

　　　例：

　　　（聽）　Good morning, Kevin. How are you?

　　　（看）　A.　I'm fine, thank you.
　　　　　　　B.　I'm in the living room.
　　　　　　　C.　My name is Kevin.

　　　　　　正確答案為 A

11. A. No, I'm lost.
　　 B. No, I know the way.
　　 C. Yes, I can guide
　　　　you.

12. A. I missed the train.
　　 B. I'm not upset.
　　 C. Yes, I was.

13. A. No. I'm going to fly.
　　 B. No. I have a ticket.
　　 C. No. I'll take a taxi.

14. A. How do you do?
　　 B. I'll have mine
　　　　well-done.
　　 C. How about seven?

15. A. The door is to your
   right.
   B. It's 2556-9898.
   C. It's in Taipei.

16. A. There is a mirror
   behind you.
   B. It's not looking at
   you.
   C. The hat is in the
   closet.

17. A. The shop is only two
   kilometers from here.
   B. About 15 minutes.
   C. I like ham, cheese
   and pineapple pizza.

18. A. I did it all except for
   English.
   B. Yes. I cleaned the
   living room and
   bathroom.
   C. I usually leave work
   at 6:00.

19. A. No, I prefer hot
   weather.
   B. No, I like sunny days.
   C. No, I wish it were
   drier.

20. A. Yes, I had a slice.
   B. No. I shared it with
   Tina.
   C. No, I did.

請 翻 頁 ⫸

第三部份： 簡短對話

本部份共 10 題，每題錄音機會播出一段對話及一個相關的問題，每題播出兩次，聽後請從試題冊上 A、B、C 三個選項中，選出一個最適合的回答，並在答案紙上塗黑作答。

例：

（聽）(Woman) Good afternoon, …Mr. Davis?

(Man) Yes. I have an appointment with Dr. Sanders at two o'clock. My son Tommy has a fever.

(Woman) Oh, that's too bad. Well, please have a seat, Mr. Davis. Dr. Sanders will be right with you.

Question: Where did this conversation take place?

（看）A. In a post office.

B. In a restaurant.

C. In a doctor's office.

正確答案為 C

21. A. She has not read the letter yet.

   B. She does not know Brian.

   C. She does not know who the letter is from.

22. A. Erase his mistake.

   B. Cross out his mistake.

   C. Get a new pen.

23. A. A house with big bedrooms.

   B. A three-bedroom house.

   C. A small house in a large, empty space.

24. A. One dose of two pills every six hours.

   B. Only two unless he has an upset stomach.

   C. He can take more than two if his stomach is not upset.

25. A. The woman is clumsy.

   B. There is something wrong with the cup.

   C. The woman dropped her cup.

請 翻 頁 ⫸

26. A. It is in the bathroom.
    B. It is next to the car.
    C. It is under the house.

27. A. The police took his cigarettes away.
    B. He was fined for smoking in a public place.
    C. He was scolded because he is too old to smoke.

28. A. Repair the power plant.
    B. Raise the price of electricity.
    C. Limit the amount of power people can use.

29. A. Less jam than the man has on his toast.
    B. A different kind of jam than the man has.
    C. Only jam, no toast.

30. A. Her father has not decided yet.
    B. Yes, she can.
    C. No. Her father is sleeping.

初級英語聽力檢定⑪詳解

第一部份

Look at the picture for question 1.

1. (**B**) What is the man looking at?

A. Avenue Street.

B. A city map.

C. It's a notebook.

* ***look at***… 看…   avenue〔'ævə,nju〕*n.* 大道
street〔strit〕*n.* 街道   city〔'sɪtɪ〕*n.* 城市
map〔mæp〕*n.* 地圖   notebook〔'not,bʊk〕*n.* 筆記本

Look at the picture for question 2.

2. (**B**) What do they want to see?

A. It is a big tent.

B. A parrot.

C. They will line up.

* tent〔tɛnt〕*n.* 帳棚   parrot〔'pærət〕*n.* 鸚鵡
line up 排隊

Look at the picture for question 3.

3. (**A**) What did the driver give the man?

A. Some money.   B. Some advice.

C. His car.

* driver〔'draɪvɚ〕*n.* 駕駛人   give〔gɪv〕*v.* 給
advice〔əd'vaɪs〕*n.* 忠告

Look at the picture for question 4.

4. (**C**) What is his hobby?

    A. It is a stamp.

    B. He likes writing letters.

    C. He enjoys collecting stamps.

    * hobby〔ˈhɑbɪ〕*n.* 嗜好　　stamp〔stæmp〕*n.* 郵票
    like〔laɪk〕*v.* 喜歡　　write〔raɪt〕*v.* 寫
    letter〔ˈlɛtɚ〕*n.* 信　　enjoy〔ɪnˈdʒɔɪ〕*v.* 喜歡；享受
    collect〔kəˈlɛkt〕*v.* 收集

Look at the picture for question 5.

5. (**C**) How is the soup?

    A. He is blowing it.

    B. With a spoon.

    C. It is hot.

    * soup〔sup〕*n.* 湯　　blow〔blo〕*v.* 吹
    with〔wɪθ〕*prep.* 用　　spoon〔spun〕*n.* 湯匙
    hot〔hɑt〕*adj.* 熱的

Look at the picture for question 6.

6. (**A**) Who does the man want to talk to?

    A. His girlfriend.　　B. His telephone.

    C. His mother.

    * want〔wɑnt〕*v.* 想要　　***talk to*** … 和…說話
    girlfriend〔ˈgɝl͵frɛnd〕*n.* 女朋友
    telephone〔ˈtɛlə͵fon〕*n.* 電話

Look at the picture for question 7.

7. (**C**) What is the problem?

    A. It is a train.

    B. They are friends.

    C. It is too noisy.

    * problem〔'prɑbləm〕*n.* 問題   train〔tren〕*n.* 火車
    noisy〔'nɔɪzɪ〕*adj.* 吵雜的

Look at the picture for question 8.

8. (**C**) What do they wear to school?

    A. They must carry their books.

    B. Four of them are going to school.

    C. They have uniforms on.

    * wear〔wɛr〕*v.* 穿   must〔mʌst〕*aux.* 必須
    carry〔'kærɪ〕*v.* 攜帶   ***have ~on*** 穿戴著（衣物）
    uniform〔'junə,fɔrm〕*n.* 制服

Look at the picture for question 9.

9. (**B**) What is the old woman holding?

    A. She is a fortuneteller.

    B. The young girl's hand.

    C. It is a ball.

    * hold〔hold〕*v.* 抓住；握著
    fortuneteller〔'fɔrtʃən,tɛlə〕*n.* 算命師（= *fortune-teller*）
    young〔jʌŋ〕*adj.* 年輕的   ball〔bɔl〕*n.* 球

Look at the picture for question 10.

10. (**B**) What is the boy doing?

     A. In a tree.

     B. Hanging.

     C. It's a branch.

     * hang〔hæŋ〕*v.* 懸掛；吊

       branch〔bræntʃ〕*n.* 樹枝

第二部份

11. (**B**) Do you need someone to guide you up the mountain?

     A. No, I'm lost.

     B. No, I know the way.

     C. Yes, I can guide you.

     * need〔nid〕*v.* 需要

       someone〔'sʌm,wʌn〕*pron.* 某人

       guide〔gaɪd〕*v.* 引導   up〔ʌp〕*prep.* 上去…

       mountain〔'maʊntn̩〕*n.* 山   lost〔lɔst〕*adj.* 迷路的

       know〔no〕*v.* 知道   way〔we〕*n.* 路

12. (**A**) Why were you absent today?

     A. I missed the train.

     B. I'm not upset.

     C. Yes, I was.

     * absent〔'æbsn̩t〕*adj.* 缺席的

       miss〔mɪs〕*v.* 錯過

       upset〔ʌp'sɛt〕*adj.* 不高興的；心煩的

13. (**C**) Do you need a ride to the airport?

    A. No. I'm going to fly.

    B. No. I have a ticket.

    C. No. I'll take a taxi.

    * ride〔raɪd〕*n.* 搭乘；搭便車

    airport〔'ɛr͵port〕*n.* 機場

    fly〔flaɪ〕*v.* 搭飛機（三態變化為：fly-flew-flown）

    ticket〔'tɪkɪt〕*n.* 票

    take〔tek〕*v.* 搭乘（交通工具）

    taxi〔'tæksɪ〕*n.* 計程車

14. (**C**) Let's arrange to meet later.

    A. How do you do?

    B. I'll have mine well-done.

    C. How about seven?

    * let's〔lɛts〕讓我們～吧

    arrange〔ə'rendʒ〕*v.* 安排

    meet〔mit〕*v.* 見面（三態變化為：meet-met-met）

    later〔'letɚ〕*adv.* 待會；稍後

    How do you do? 你好嗎？（初次見面的問候語）

    mine〔maɪn〕*pron.* 我的（東西）（在此表牛排類的食物）

    well-done〔'wɛl'dʌn〕*adj.* 全熟的

    I'll have mine well-done. 我的要全熟。

    How about seven? 七點怎麼樣；七點好不好？

15. (**A**) Where is the entrance?

    A. The door is to your right.

    B. It's 2556-9898.

    C. It's in Taipei.

    * entrance〔'ɛntrəns〕 *v.* 入口   to〔tu〕*prep.* 在…方
      right〔raɪt〕*n.* 右邊   Taipei〔'taɪ'pe〕*n.* 台北

16. (**A**) How does this hat look on me?

    A. There is a mirror behind you.

    B. It's not looking at you.

    C. The hat is in the closet.

    * hat〔hæt〕*n.* 帽子   look〔lʊk〕*v.* 看起來
      on〔ɑn〕*prep.* 在…身上   mirror〔'mɪrɚ〕*n.* 鏡子
      behind〔bɪ'haɪnd〕*prep.* 在…後面
      closet〔'klɑzɪt〕*n.* 衣櫥

17. (**B**) How long should I bake the pizza?

    A. The shop is only two kilometers from here.

    B. About 15 minutes.

    C. I like ham, cheese and pineapple pizza.

    * ***How long ~?*** ~多久？   should〔ʃʊd〕*aux.* 應該
      bake〔bek〕*v.* 烘烤   pizza〔'pitsə〕*n.* 披薩
      shop〔ʃɑp〕*n.* 商店   only〔'onlɪ〕*adv.* 只不過~而已
      kilometer〔'kɪlə,mitɚ〕*n.* 公里   from〔frɑm〕*prep.* 離…
      about〔ə'baʊt〕*adv.* 大約   minute〔'mɪnɪt〕*n.* 分鐘
      ham〔hæm〕*n.* 火腿   cheese〔tʃiz〕*n.* 起司
      pineapple〔'paɪn,æpl̩〕*n.* 鳳梨

18. (**B**) Did you finish the housework?

    A. I did it all except for English.

    B. Yes. I cleaned the living room and bathroom.

    C. I usually leave work at 6:00.

    * finish〔'fɪnɪʃ〕v. 完成

      housework〔'haʊs,wɝk〕n. 家事

      except〔ɪk'sɛpt〕prep. 除了…之外（兩者性質不同時）

      except for… 除了…之外（兩者性質相同時）

      clean〔klin〕v. 打掃　*living room* 客廳

      bathroom〔'bæθ,rum〕n. 浴室

      usually〔'juʒʊəlɪ〕adv. 通常

      leave〔liv〕v. 離開

      work〔wɝk〕n. 工作　*leave work* 下班

19. (**C**) Do you like humid weather?

    A. No, I prefer hot weather.

    B. No, I like sunny days.

    C. No, I wish it were drier.

    * humid〔'hjumɪd〕adj. 潮濕的

      weather〔'wɛðɚ〕n. 天氣

      prefer〔prɪ'fɝ〕v. 比較喜歡　　hot〔hɑt〕adj. 熱的

      sunny〔'sʌnɪ〕adj. 晴朗的　　wish〔wɪʃ〕v. 希望

      were〔wɝ〕aux. are 的過去式（在與現在事實相反的

        假設法中，無論主詞單複數，一律用 were。）

      drier〔'draɪɚ〕adj. 較乾的（dry 的比較級）

20. (**B**) Did you eat the entire cake?

    A. Yes, I had a slice.

    B. No. I shared it with Tina.

    C. No, I did.

    * entire〔ɪn'taɪr〕*adj.* 整個的　　have〔hæv〕*v.* 吃
    slice〔slaɪs〕*n.* 片　　share〔ʃɛr〕*v.* 分享

第三部份

21. (**A**) M：What's in the envelope?

    W：It's a letter from Brian.

    M：Oh, how is he?

    W：I'll tell you as soon as I know.

    Question：What does the woman mean?

    A. She has not read the letter yet.

    B. She does not know Brian.

    C. She does not know who the letter is from.

    * envelope〔'ɛnvə,lop〕*n.* 信封　　letter〔'lɛtɚ〕*n.* 信
    from〔frɑm〕*prep.* 從…來的
    oh〔o〕*interj.* 喔（因驚訝所發出的感嘆）
    ~ as soon as… 一…就~　　mean〔min〕*v.* 意思是
    yet〔jɛt〕*adv.* 尚（未）（用於否定句）

22. (**B**) M：Uh-oh. I made a spelling mistake.

    W：Here's an eraser.

    M：That won't help. I'm using a pen.

    Question：What can the man do?

A. Erase his mistake.

B. Cross out his mistake.

C. Get a new pen.

* uh-oh〔ˋʌˋo〕interj. 唔哦（遭遇問題時的感嘆語）
spelling〔ˋspɛlɪŋ〕n. 拼字　　mistake〔məˋstek〕n. 錯誤
make a mistake 犯錯　　**Here is ~.** 這是~。
eraser〔ɪˋresɚ〕n. 橡皮擦
That won't help. 那沒有幫助。　　use〔juz〕v. 使用
pen〔pɛn〕n. 筆（原子筆、鋼筆等）
erase〔ɪˋres〕v. 擦掉　　**cross out** （用筆）劃掉；刪去
get〔gɛt〕v. 買

23. (**B**) M：Have you had any luck finding a house?

W：No. Everything we've seen is too small.

M：How much space do you need?

W：We need at least three bedrooms.

Question：What does the woman want?

A. A house with big bedrooms.

B. A three-bedroom house.

C. A small house in a large, empty space.

* luck〔lʌk〕n. 好運　　find〔faɪnd〕v. 找
everything〔ˋɛvrɪˏθɪŋ〕pron. 一切事物
small〔smɔl〕adj. 小的　　space〔spes〕n. 空間
need〔nid〕v. 需要　　**at least** 至少
bedroom〔ˋbɛdˏrum〕n. 臥室
A three-bedroom house. 有三間臥室的房子。
large〔lɑrdʒ〕adj. 大的　　empty〔ˋɛmptɪ〕adj. 空的

24. (**A**)　M：Will these pills help my headache?

　　　　　W：They should, but take no more than two in a six-hour period.

　　　　　M：Only two?

　　　　　W：Yes.　An overdose could cause an upset stomach.

　　　　　Question：How many pills should the man take?

　　　　A.　One dose of two pills every six hours.

　　　　B.　Only two unless he has an upset stomach.

　　　　C.　He can take more than two if his stomach is not upset.

　　　　* pill〔pɪl〕*n.* 藥丸　　help〔hɛlp〕*v.* 有助於治療

　　　　　headache〔'hɛd,ek〕*n.* 頭痛

　　　　　should〔ʃʊd〕*aux.* 應該　　take〔tek〕*v.* 吃（藥）

　　　　　no more than 不超過　　period〔'pɪrɪəd〕*n.* 期間

　　　　　in a six-hour period 在六小時期間內

　　　　　only〔'onlɪ〕*adv.* 只有

　　　　　overdose〔,ovɚ'dos〕*n.* 服藥過量

　　　　　could〔kʊd〕*aux.* 可能（can 的過去式，語氣比 can 委婉）

　　　　　cause〔kɔz〕*v.* 引起

　　　　　upset〔ʌp'sɛt〕*adj.* （腸胃）不舒服的

　　　　　stomach〔'stʌmək〕*n.* 胃　　dose〔dos〕*n.* 一劑（藥）

　　　　　unless〔ʌn'lɛs〕*conj.* 除非

25. (**B**)　M：Hey, you're dripping coffee all over the floor.

　　　　　W：Oh, how clumsy of me.

　　　　　M：It's not you.　There's a hole in the cup.

　　　　　Question：Why is there coffee on the floor?

A. The woman is clumsy.

B. There is something wrong with the cup.

C. The woman dropped her cup.

* hey〔he〕*interj.* 嘿（引起注意、表驚訝等的叫聲）

drip〔drɪp〕*v.* （液體）滴落

all over 遍及　　　floor〔flor〕*n.* 地板

clumsy〔ˈklʌmzɪ〕*adj.* 笨拙的

hole〔hol〕*n.* 洞

There is something wrong with… …出了毛病；…有問題

drop〔drɑp〕*v.* 使掉落

26. (**C**) M: Do you have a washing machine?

W: Of course.

M: Where is it?

W: It's in the basement.

Question: Where is the washing machine?

A. It is in the bathroom.

B. It is next to the car.

C. It is under the house.

* machine〔məˈʃin〕*n.* 機器

washing machine 洗衣機　　***of course*** 當然

basement〔ˈbesmənt〕*n.* 地下室

bathroom〔ˈbæθˌrum〕*n.* 浴室

next to… 在…旁邊

under〔ˈʌndɚ〕*prep.* 在…之下

27. (**A**) M：Alex got in trouble with the police last night.

W：What happened?

M：They saw him smoking and confiscated his cigarettes.

W：Well, he's not allowed to smoke at his age.

Question：What happened to Alex?

A. The police took his cigarettes away.

B. He was fined for smoking in a public place.

C. He was scolded because he is too old to smoke.

* trouble〔'trʌbḷ〕 *n.* 麻煩

get in trouble with… 　與…有了麻煩（糾紛）

police〔pə'lis〕 *n.* 警方　　***last night*** 昨天晚上

happen〔'hæpən〕 *v.* 發生

see〔si〕 *v.* 看見（三態變化爲：see-saw-seen）

smoke〔smok〕 *v.* 抽煙

confiscate〔'kɑnfɪsˌket〕 *v.* 沒收；充公

cigarette〔ˌsɪgə'rɛt, 'sɪgəˌrɛt〕 *n.* 香煙

allow〔ə'laʊ〕 *v.* 允許　　age〔edʒ〕 *n.* 年齡

at his age 在他這個年齡時

take away 拿走　　***be fine for*** ~ 因～被科以罰金

public〔'pʌblɪk〕 *adj.* 公共的

place〔ples〕 *n.* 地方；場所

scold〔skold〕 *v.* 責罵

because〔bɪ'kɔz〕 *conj.* 因爲

too…to ~ 太…以致不能～

28. (**C**) M: The power plant was severely damaged.

W: Yes, and now there is a shortage of electricity.

M: Do you think the government will ration it?

W: Yes, I think they will have to.

Question: What does the woman say the government
will do?

A. Repair the power plant.

B. Raise the price of electricity.

C. Limit the amount of power people can use.

* power〔'pauɚ〕 n. 電力　　plant〔plænt〕 n. 工廠

　power plant 發電廠　　severely〔sə'vɪrlɪ〕 adv. 嚴重地

　damage〔'dæmɪdʒ〕 v. 損害

　shortage〔'ʃɔrtɪdʒ〕 n. 不足；短缺

　electricity〔ɪˌlɛk'trɪsətɪ〕 n. 電

　think〔θɪŋk〕 v. 認為（三態變化為：think-thought-thought）

　government〔'gʌvənmənt〕 n. 政府

　ration〔'ræʃən〕 v. 配給　　repair〔rɪ'pɛr〕 v. 修理

　raise〔rez〕 v. 提高　　price〔praɪs〕 n. 價格

　limit〔'lɪmɪt〕 v. 限制　　amount〔ə'maunt〕 n. 數量

29. (**A**) M: Would you like some jam on your toast?

W: Yes, please, but not like yours.

M: You want a different kind of jam?

W: No, strawberry is fine, but I don't want such a
thick layer.

Question: What does the woman want?

A. Less jam than the man has on his toast.

B. A different kind of jam than the man has.

C. Only jam, no toast.

* ***Would you like～?*** 你要不要～？
  jam〔dʒæm〕*n.* 果醬　　toast〔tost〕*n.* 吐司
  Yes, please*.* 好，麻煩你。（用以答應別人的勸誘）
  like〔laɪk〕*prep.* 像
  yours〔jʊrz〕*pron.* 你的（東西）（在此指「你吐司上的果醬」）
  different〔'dɪfərənt〕*adj.* 不同的　　kind〔kaɪnd〕*n.* 種類
  strawberry〔'strɔ,bɛrɪ〕*n.* 草莓　　fine〔faɪn〕*adj.* 很好的
  such〔sʌtʃ〕*adj.* 如此的　　thick〔θɪk〕*adj.* 厚的
  layer〔'leɚ〕*n.* 一層　　less〔lɛs〕*adj.* 較少的

30.（ **B** ）M：Did you ask your father if you could borrow the car?

W：Yes, I did.

M：What did he say?

W：He didn't say anything, but he nodded.

Question：Can the woman borrow the car?

A. Her father has not decided yet.

B. Yes, she can.

C. No.　Her father is sleeping.

* ask〔æsk〕*v.* 問　　if〔ɪf〕*conj.* 是否
  could〔kʊd〕*aux.* 可以（can 的過去式）
  borrow〔'bɑro〕*v.* 借（入）
  anything〔'ɛnɪ,θɪŋ〕*pron.* 任何事
  nod〔nɑd〕*v.* 點頭　　decide〔dɪ'saɪd〕*v.* 決定
  yet〔jɛt〕*adv.* 尚（未）（用於否定句）
  sleep〔slip〕*v.* 睡覺

全民英語能力分級檢定測驗
初級測驗⑫

　　本測驗分三部份，全為三選一之選擇題，每部份各 10 題，共 30 題，作答時間約 20 分鐘。

第一部份：看圖辨義

　　　　　本部份共 10 題，試題冊上每題有一個圖片，請聽錄音機播出一個相關的問題，與 A、B、C 三個英語敘述後，選一個與所看到圖片最相符的答案，並在答案紙上相對的圓圈內塗黑作答。每題播出一遍，問題及選項均不印在試題冊上。

例：（看）

NT$80　　NT$50

（聽）

Look at the picture.　How much is the hamburger?

　　A. It's eighty dollars.
　　B. It's fifty-five dollars.
　　C. It's eighteen dollars.

正確答案為 A

Question 1

Question 2

Question 3

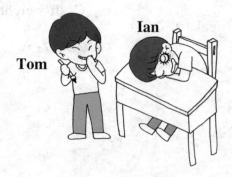

Tom　Ian

Question 4

Question 5

請 翻 頁 ⟹

Question 6

Question 7

Question 8

Question 9

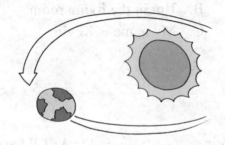

Question 10

請翻頁 ▯▭▷

第二部份： 問答

本部份共 10 題，每題錄音機會播出一個問句或直述句，每題播出一次，聽後請從試題冊上 A、B、C 三個選項中，選出一個最適合的回答或回應，並在答案紙上塗黑作答。

例：

（聽） Good morning, Kevin. How are you?

（看） A. I'm fine, thank you.
　　　 B. I'm in the living room.
　　　 C. My name is Kevin.

正確答案為 A

11. A. It's a circle.
　　 B. It closes the door.
　　 C. It's on the wall.

12. A. No. What happened?
　　 B. The late news is on at 10 p.m.
　　 C. No, it's not here.

13. A. I'll have a cheeseburger, fries and a Coke.
　　 B. No, I don't have any money.
　　 C. I'd like some juice if you have any.

14. A. No, but I'll be ready in
ten minutes.

    B. Yes, I swim five times
a week.

    C. Only about 200 meters.

15. A. No. Who told you?

    B. It was a knock on the
door.

    C. Yes, I have it here
somewhere.

16. A. Yes. You'd better give
him some water to drink.

    B. Yes, so don't touch it.

    C. Yes. Let's turn on the
air conditioner.

17. A. Yes, I can do 60
words per minute.

    B. Yes, it's a poodle.

    C. Yes, I often run in the
morning.

18. A. Yes, I am.

    B. Yes, he's very
friendly.

    C. No, it's not very
bright.

19. A. I've been feeling
much better.

    B. She's fine, thank
you.

    C. I got an A in class
yesterday.

20. A. I'm going to wash
his car for NT$100.

    B. He helped me to
finish my math
homework.

    C. Because I was
being too noisy.

請 翻 頁 ▐▐⟹

第三部份： 簡短對話

本部份共 10 題，每題錄音機會播出一段對話及一個相關的問題，每題播出兩次，聽後請從試題冊上 A、B、C 三個選項中，選出一個最適合的回答，並在答案紙上塗黑作答。

例：

(聽) (Woman) Good afternoon, …Mr. Davis?

(Man) Yes. I have an appointment with Dr. Sanders at two o'clock. My son Tommy has a fever.

(Woman) Oh, that's too bad. Well, please have a seat, Mr. Davis. Dr. Sanders will be right with you.

Question: Where did this conversation take place?

(看) A. In a post office.

B. In a restaurant.

C. In a doctor's office.

正確答案為 C

21. A. She thinks it was very
realistic.
   B. She really liked it.
   C. She thought it was
not funny.

22. A. He will probably not
come.
   B. He might arrive in a
little while.
   C. He will come too late.

23. A. The man enjoys
playing the lottery.
   B. The man often wins
the lottery, but the
woman doesn't.
   C. The woman thinks
winning the lottery is
too much bother.

24. A. The man and the
woman both liked
the book.
   B. The woman did not
enjoy the second
book.
   C. The man enjoys
reading more than
the woman does.

25. A. As many as she can
find.
   B. Less than a dozen.
   C. Twelve or more.

請 翻 頁 ▶

26. A. They are from an
　　 elementary school.
　 B. They don't go to
　　 school anymore.
　 C. They go to a junior
　　 high school.

27. A. The woman left her
　　 notebook in the
　　 science class.
　 B. The woman never
　　 takes notes in class.
　 C. The woman was not
　　 able to take notes.

28. A. She walked to school.
　 B. She stayed in the school.
　 C. She climbed a hill.

29. A. She doesn't like
　　 hobbies.
　 B. She enjoys painting.
　 C. She has no free time
　　 for hobbies.

30. A. There is a lot of soup in
　　 the bowl.
　 B. The bowl is very hot.
　 C. She has only two hands.

初級英語聽力檢定⑫詳解

第一部份

Look at the picture for question 1.

1. (**C**) What is on the boy's feet?

　　A. No, he is standing on one foot.

　　B. He is kicking.　　C. His feet are bare.

　*　feet〔fit〕*n. pl.* 腳（foot〔fʊt〕的複數）

　　stand〔stænd〕*v.* 站　***stand on one foot*** 用一隻腳站著

　　kick〔kɪk〕*v.* 踢　　bare〔bɛr〕*adj.* 赤裸的

Look at the picture for question 2.

2. (**A**) What is in the boy's hand?

　　A. A button.　　B. Baseball.

　　C. His shirt.

　*　hand〔hænd〕*n.* 手　　button〔'bʌtn̩〕*n.* 鈕扣

　　baseball〔'bes,bɔl〕*n.* 棒球　　shirt〔ʃɝt〕*n.* 襯衫

Look at the picture for question 3.

3. (**B**) What did Tom do?

　　A. He is laughing.　　B. He drew on Ian.

　　C. They were fighting.

　*　laugh〔læf〕*v.* 笑

　　draw〔drɔ〕*v.* 畫（三態變化爲：draw-drew-drawn）

　　fight〔faɪt〕*v.* 打架（三態變化爲：fight-fought-fought）

Look at the picture for question 4.

4. (**C**) Who is the woman?

  A. He is tired.

  B. She is carrying the boy.

  C. She is his mother.

  * tired〔taɪrd〕*adj.* 疲倦的　　carry〔'kærɪ〕*v.* 抱著

Look at the picture for question 5.

5. (**A**) What will the shoe look like?

  A. It will be shiny.

  B. Because his shoes are dirty.

  C. He is brushing it.

  * shoe〔ʃu〕*n.* 鞋子　　***look like*** ~ 看起來像~

  shiny〔'ʃaɪnɪ〕*adj.* 發亮的

  because〔bɪ'kɔz〕*conj.* 因為

  dirty〔'dɝtɪ〕*adj.* 髒的　　brush〔brʌʃ〕*v.* 刷

Look at the picture for question 6.

6. (**A**) What will they eat?

  A. Barbecue.

  B. They will eat outside.

  C. They will all eat it.

  * barbecue〔'bɑrbɪˌkju〕*n.* 烤肉（= *Bar-B-Q*）

  outside〔'aʊt'saɪd〕*adv.* 在外面

  all〔ɔl〕*pron.* 全部的人

Look at the picture for question 7.

7. (**A**) Where is the girl?

    A. She is on the stairs.

    B. She is upstairs.

    C. She is climbing.

    * stairs〔stɛrz〕*n. pl.* 樓梯

       upstairs〔'ʌp'stɛrz〕*adv.* 在樓上   climb〔klaɪm〕*v.* 爬

Look at the picture for question 8.

8. (**C**) What will they do?

    A. They won the lottery.

    B. They will get married.

    C. They will listen to music.

    * win〔wɪn〕*v.* 贏（三態變化為：win-won-won）

       lottery〔'lɑtərɪ〕*n.* 彩券   married〔'mærɪd〕*adj.* 結婚的

       get〔gɛt〕*v.* 成為…狀態   ***get married*** 結婚

       listen to 聽   music〔'mjuzɪk〕*n.* 音樂

Look at the picture for question 9.

9. (**B**) What does the Earth do?

    A. It likes the sun.

    B. It goes around the sun.

    C. It follows the sun.

    * earth〔ɝθ〕*n.* 地球   like〔laɪk〕*v.* 喜歡

       sun〔sʌn〕*n.* 太陽   ***go around*** 繞著…運行

       follow〔'fɑlo〕*v.* 跟隨

Look at the picture for question 10.

10. (**B**) What is the man looking for?

  A. A bus.

  B. Some coins.

  C. His pocket.

  * ***look for*** 尋找 coin〔kɔɪn〕*n.* 硬幣

   pocket〔'pɑkɪt〕*n.* 口袋

第二部份

11. (**B**) What is the function of this button?

  A. It's a circle.

  B. It closes the door.

  C. It's on the wall.

  * function〔'fʌŋkʃən〕*n.* 功能 button〔'bʌtn̩〕*n.* 按鈕

   circle〔'sɝkl̩〕*n.* 圓圈 close〔kloz〕*v.* 關上

   wall〔wɔl〕*n.* 牆壁

12. (**A**) Have you heard the latest news?

  A. No. What happened?

  B. The late news is on at 10 p.m.

  C. No, it's not here.

  * hear〔hɪr〕*v.* 聽說；聽見

   latest〔'letɪst〕*adj.* 最新的；最近的

   news〔njuz〕*n.* 新聞；消息 happen〔'hæpən〕*v.* 發生

   late〔let〕*adj.* 入夜之後的 on〔ɑn〕*adv.* (節目)上演中

   p.m.〔'pi'ɛm〕*adv.* 下午 (= *P.M.*)

   here〔hɪr〕*adv.* 在這裡

13. (**C**)　Can I offer you something to drink?

A.　I'll have a cheeseburger, fries and a Coke.

B.　No, I don't have any money.

C.　I'd like some juice if you have any.

* offer〔'ɔfɚ〕 v. 提供　　something〔'sʌmθɪŋ〕 pron. 某物
drink〔drɪŋk〕 v. 喝
cheeseburger〔'tʃiz,bɝgɚ〕 n. 起司漢堡
fries〔fraɪz〕 n. pl. 薯條（ = *French fries*）
Coke〔kok〕 n. 可口可樂（ = *Coca-Cola*）
would like 想要（ = *want*）　　juice〔dʒus〕 n. 果汁

14. (**C**)　How far can you swim in five minutes?

A.　No, but I'll be ready in ten minutes.

B.　Yes, I swim five times a week.

C.　Only about 200 meters.

* *How far ~ ?*　～多遠？　　swim〔swɪm〕 v. 游泳
minute〔'mɪnɪt〕 n. 分鐘　　*in five minutes* 在五分鐘內
ready〔'rɛdɪ〕 adj. 準備好的　　time〔taɪm〕 n. 次數
five times a week 一星期五次　　only〔'onlɪ〕 adv. 只有
about〔ə'baʊt〕 adv. 大約　　meter〔'mitɚ〕 n. 公尺

15. (**B**)　Did you hear that sound?

A.　No.　Who told you?

B.　It was a knock on the door.

C.　Yes, I have it here somewhere.

* sound〔saʊnd〕 n. 聲音　　knock〔nak〕 n. 敲門聲
somewhere〔'sʌm,whɛr〕 adv. 在某處

16. (**B**) Is the pot hot?

    A. Yes. You'd better give him some water to drink.

    B. Yes, so don't touch it.

    C. Yes. Let's turn on the air conditioner.

    * pot〔pɑt〕*n.* 鍋；壺　　hot〔hɑt〕*adj.* 熱的

      had better V. 最好～　　give〔gɪv〕*v.* 給

      water〔'wɔtɚ〕*n.* 水　　so〔so〕*adv.* 所以

      touch〔tʌtʃ〕*v.* 觸摸　　let's〔lɛts〕讓我們～吧

      turn on 打開（電器）

      air conditioner 空調；冷氣機

17. (**C**) Do you jog?

    A. Yes, I can do 60 words per minute.

    B. Yes, it's a poodle.

    C. Yes, I often run in the morning.

    * jog〔dʒɑg〕*v.* 慢跑　　word〔wɝd〕*n.* 字

      per〔pɚ〕*prep.* 每一　　minute〔'mɪnɪt〕*n.* 分鐘

      poodle〔'pudl̩〕*n.* 貴賓狗　　often〔'ɔfən〕*adv.* 經常

      run〔rʌn〕*v.* 跑

18. (**A**) Are you frightened of the dentist?

    A. Yes, I am.

    B. Yes, he's very friendly.

    C. No, it's not very bright.

    * frightened〔'fraɪtn̩d〕*adj.* 害怕的 <*of*>

      dentist〔'dɛntɪst〕*n.* 牙醫

      friendly〔'frɛndlɪ〕*adj.* 友善的

      bright〔braɪt〕*adj.* 明亮的

19. (**A**) How has your health been?

    A. I've been feeling much better.

    B. She's fine, thank you.

    C. I got an A in class yesterday.

    * health〔hɛlθ〕*n.* 健康

    How has your health been? 你的身體最近還好嗎？

    feel〔fil〕*v.* 覺得　　*much better* 好很多

    fine〔faɪn〕*adj.* 很好的　　get〔gɛt〕*v.* 得到（成績）

    in class 在課堂上

20. (**A**) What did he hire you to do?

    A. I'm going to wash his car for NT$100.

    B. He helped me to finish my math homework.

    C. Because I was being too noisy.

    * hire〔haɪr〕*v.* 雇用　　help〔hɛlp〕*v.* 幫助

    finish〔'fɪnɪʃ〕*v.* 完成；做完

    math〔mæθ〕*n.* 數學（= *mathematics*）

    homework〔'hom‚wɝk〕*n.* 家庭作業

    because〔bɪ'kɔz〕*conj.* 因為　　noisy〔'nɔɪzɪ〕*adj.* 吵鬧的

第三部份

21. (**C**) M：Did you like the movie?

    W：Not really.

    M：But it's one of the best comedies of the year!

    W：I didn't see the humor in it.

    Question：What did the woman think of the movie?

A. She thinks it was very realistic.

B. She really liked it.

C. She thought it was not funny.

* movie〔'muvɪ〕n. 電影　　***Not really.*** 其實不喜歡。
  best〔bɛst〕adj. 最好的　　comedy〔'kamədɪ〕n. 喜劇
  see〔si〕v. 看見；了解 (三態變化為：see-saw-seen)
  humor〔'hjumɚ〕n. 幽默　　***think of*** 認為
  realistic〔ˌriə'lɪstɪk〕adj. 實際的；寫實的
  really〔'riəlɪ〕adv. 真地　　funny〔'fʌnɪ〕adj. 好笑的

22. (**B**) M：Is Jack here yet?

W：No, he isn't.

M：Do you think he will come later?

W：Probably.

Question：When will Jack arrive?

A. He will probably not come.

B. He might arrive in a little while.

C. He will come too late.

* here〔hɪr〕adv. 到這裡
  yet〔jɛt〕adv. 已經 (用於疑問句)
  later〔'letɚ〕adv. 待會；稍後
  probably〔'prabəblɪ〕adv. 可能
  arrive〔ə'raɪv〕v. 抵達
  might〔maɪt〕aux. 可能
  while〔hwaɪl〕n. 短暫的時間
  in a little while 再過不久　　late〔let〕adv. 晚

23. (**A**)　M：Let's pick some numbers for the lottery.

　　　　　W：Why bother?　We'll never win.

　　　　　M：It's just for fun.

　　　　　Question：Which of the following is true?

　　　　　A. The man enjoys playing the lottery.

　　　　　B. The man often wins the lottery, but the woman

　　　　　　　doesn't.

　　　　　C. The woman thinks winning the lottery is too much

　　　　　　　bother.

*　pick〔pɪk〕*v.* 挑選　　　number〔'nʌmbɚ〕*n.* 數字

　　lottery〔'lɑtərɪ〕*n.* 彩券

　　bother〔'bɑðɚ〕*v.* 煩惱；費事　*n.* 麻煩

　　Why bother? 幹嘛這麼麻煩？

　　never〔'nɛvɚ〕*adv.* 從未

　　win〔wɪn〕*v.* 贏（三態變化爲：win-won-won）

　　We'll never win. 我們不會中的。

　　just〔dʒʌst〕*adv.* 只是…而已　　fun〔fʌn〕*n.* 樂趣

　　It's just for fun. 只是好玩而已。

　　which〔hwɪtʃ〕*pron.* 哪一個

　　following〔'fɑləwɪŋ〕*adj.* 下列的

　　the following 下列的物（人）

　　true〔tru〕*adj.* 正確的

　　enjoy〔ɪn'dʒɔɪ〕*v.* 喜歡；享受

　　play〔ple〕*v.* 玩；賭

24. (**A**) M：How did you like that novel?

W：I enjoyed it very much.

M：So did I, but the second one is even better.

Question：Which of the following is true?

A. The man and the woman both liked the book.

B. The woman did not enjoy the second book.

C. The man enjoys reading more than the woman does.

* ***How did you like～?*** 你覺得～怎麼樣；你喜歡～嗎？
novel〔ˋnɑvl̩〕*n.* 小說
enjoy〔ɪnˋdʒɔɪ〕*v.* 喜歡；享受
So did I. 我也是。
second〔ˋsɛkənd〕*adj.* 第二的
even〔ˋivən〕*adv.* 甚至
better〔ˋbɛtɚ〕*adj.* 較好的（good 的比較級）
both〔boθ〕*pron.* 兩者　　***more than***… 更甚於…

25. (**C**) M：I need some tomatoes to make the spaghetti sauce.

W：I'll go buy some. How many do you need?

M：At least a dozen.

Question：How many tomatoes will the woman buy?

A. As many as she can find.

B. Less than a dozen.

C. Twelve or more.

* need〔nid〕v. 需要　　tomato〔tə'meto〕n. 蕃茄

make〔mek〕v. 做

spaghetti〔spə'gɛtɪ〕n. 義大利麵

sauce〔sɔs〕n. 調味醬

go buy 去買（＝ go to buy＝ go and buy ）

some〔sʌm〕pron. 一些（在此指「一些蕃茄」）

at least 至少　　dozen〔'dʌzn̩〕n. 一打

as many as ~ 同~一樣多　　find〔faɪnd〕v. 找到

As many as she can find. 她能找到多少就買多少。

less than… 少於…　　more〔mor〕adj. 更多的

26. (**C**) M：Are those students from around here?

W：Yes, but they don't go to school here anymore.

M：Why not?

W：They are former elementary school students.

Question：Where do the students go to school?

A. They are from an elementary school.

B. They don't go to school anymore.

C. They go to a junior high school.

* from〔frɑm〕prep. 來自

around〔ə'raʊnd〕prep. 在…附近

around here 在這附近

anymore〔'ɛnɪˌmor〕adv. 再也（不）（用於否定句）

Why not? 為什麼不？　　former〔'fɔrmɚ〕adj. 從前的

elementary〔ˌɛlə'mɛntərɪ〕adj. 初等的

elementary school 小學

junior high school 國中

27. (**C**) M：Can I borrow your notes from the science class?

W：Sorry, I didn't take any.

M：Why not?

W：I forgot to take a notebook with me.

Question：Which of the following is true?

A. The woman left her notebook in the science class.

B. The woman never takes notes in class.

C. The woman was not able to take notes.

* borrow〔'baro〕*v.* 借（入） note〔not〕*n.* 筆記
science〔'saɪəns〕*n.* 科學 class〔klæs〕*n.* 課
sorry〔'sɔrɪ〕*interj.* 對不起
take〔tek〕*v.* 記下；攜帶
any〔'ɛnɪ〕*pron.* 任何事物
Why not? 為什麼沒記？ forget〔fɚ'gɛt〕*v.* 忘記
notebook〔'not,bʊk〕*n.* 筆記本
take sth. with sb. 某人帶某物在身上
leave〔liv〕*v.* 遺留（三態變化為：leave-left-left）
take notes 記筆記 **be able to V.** 能夠～

28. (**C**) M：Where have you been?

W：I went for a walk.

M：Around the school?

W：No. There are some hills behind the school.

Question：What did the woman do?

A. She walked to school.

B. She stayed in the school.

C. She climbed a hill.

* ***Where have you been?*** 你去哪裡了？

go for a walk 去散步

around〔əˋraʊnd〕*prep.* 在⋯附近

hill〔hɪl〕*n.* 山丘

behind〔bɪˋhaɪnd〕*prep.* 在⋯後面

stay〔ste〕*v.* 停留　　climb〔klaɪm〕*v.* 爬

29.(**B**) M：Do you have a favorite sport?

W：No. I don't like sports very much.

M：So what do you do in your free time?

W：I like painting so I'm taking an art class.

Question：What is the woman's hobby?

A. She doesn't like hobbies.

B. She enjoys painting.

C. She has no free time for hobbies.

* favorite〔ˋfevərɪt〕*adj.* 最喜愛的

sport〔sport〕*n.* 運動　　so〔so〕*adv.* 那麼

free〔fri〕*adj.* 空閒的　　paint〔pent〕*v.* 畫畫

take〔tek〕*v.* 修（課）　　art〔ɑrt〕*adj.* 藝術的

hobby〔ˋhɑbɪ〕*n.* 嗜好

enjoy〔ɪnˋdʒɔɪ〕*v.* 喜歡；享受

30. (**A**) M：Here is your soup.

W：Thanks. The bowl is so full.

M：Be careful and hold it with both hands.

Question：Why must the woman be careful?

A. There is a lot of soup in the bowl.

B. The bowl is very hot.

C. She has only two hands.

* **Here is ～** . 這是～。　　soup〔sup〕n. 湯
bowl〔bol〕n. 碗　　so〔so〕adv. 非常
full〔fʊl〕adj. 滿的　　**be careful** 要小心
hold〔hold〕v. 抓住；拿著　　with〔wɪθ〕prep. 用
both〔boθ〕adj. 兩個的　　hand〔hænd〕n. 手
must〔mʌst〕aux. 一定　　**a lot of** 許多
hot〔hɑt〕adj. 熱的

【劉毅老師的話】

1. 練習聽力時，要先看選項，永遠保持領先。
   萬一有一條題目不會答，要立刻放棄。

2. 聽力要考滿分，就是要不斷地練習，做愈多
   題目愈好。

附錄

全民英語能力分級檢定測驗簡介

「全民英語能力分級檢定測驗」（General English Proficiency Test），簡稱「全民英檢」（GEPT），旨在提供我國各階段英語學習者一公平、可靠、具效度之英語能力評量工具，測驗對象包括在校學生及一般社會人士，可做為學習成果檢定、教學改進及公民營機構甄選人才等之參考。

本測驗為標準參照測驗（criterion-referenced test），參考當前我國英語教育體制，制定分級標準，整套系統共分五級——初級（Elementary）、中級（Intermediate）、中高級（High-Intermediate）、高級（Advanced）、優級（Superior）。每級訂有明確能力標準（詳見表一綜合能力說明），報考者可依英語能力選擇適當級數報考，每級均包含聽、說、讀、寫四項完整的測驗，通過所報考級數的能力標準即可取得該級的合格證書。各級命題設計均參考目前各階段英語教育之課程大綱及相關教材之內容分析，期能符合國內各階段英語教育的需求、反應本土的生活經驗與特色。

「**全民英語能力檢定分級測驗**」各級綜合能力説明　　《表一》

級數	綜　合　能　力	備　　　　　　　註	
初級	通過初級測驗者具有基礎英語能力，能理解和使用淺易日常用語，英語能力相當於國中畢業者。	建議下列人員宜具有該級英語能力	一般行政助理、維修技術人員、百貨業、餐飲業、旅館業或觀光景點服務人員、計程車駕駛等。
中級	通過中級測驗者具有使用簡單英語進行日常生活溝通的能力，英語能力相當於高中職畢業者。		一般行政、業務、技術、銷售人員、護理人員、旅館、飯店接待人員、總機人員、警政人員、旅遊從業人員等。
中高級	通過中高級測驗者英語能力逐漸成熟，應用的領域擴大，雖有錯誤，但無礙溝通，英語能力相當於大學非英語主修系所畢業者。		商務、企劃人員、祕書、工程師、研究助理、空服人員、航空機師、航管人員、海關人員、導遊、外事警政人員、新聞從業人員、資訊管理人員等。

級數	綜 合 能 力		備 註
高 級	通過高級測驗者英語流利順暢，僅有少許錯誤，應用能力擴及學術或專業領域，英語能力相當於國內大學英語主修系所或曾赴英語系國家大學或研究所進修並取得學位者。	建議下列人員宜具有該級英語能力	高級商務人員、協商談判人員、英語教學人員、研究人員、翻譯人員、外交人員、國際新聞從業人員等。
優 級	通過優級測驗者的英語能力接近受過高等教育之母語人士，各種場合均能使用適當策略作最有效的溝通。		專業翻譯人員、國際新聞特派人員、外交官員、協商談判主談人員等。

初級英語能力測驗簡介

I. 通過初級檢定者的英語能力

聽	説	讀	寫
能聽懂簡易的英語句子、對話及故事。	能簡單地自我介紹並以簡易英語對答；能朗讀簡易文章。	能瞭解簡易英語對話、短文、故事及書信的內容；能看懂常用的標示。	能寫簡單的英語句子及段落。

II. 測 驗 內 容

測驗項目	初 試			複 試
	聽力測驗	閱讀能力測驗	寫作能力測驗	口説能力測驗
總題數	30	35	16	18
作答時間／分鐘	約 20	35	40	約 10
測驗內容	看圖辨義 問答 簡短對話	詞彙和結構 段落填空 閱讀理解	單句寫作 段落寫作	複誦 朗讀句子與短文 回答問題

　　聽力及閱讀能力測驗成績採標準計分方式，60分為平均數，滿分 120分。寫作及口說能力測驗成績採整體式評分，使用級分制，分為 0～5 級分，再轉換成百分制。各項成績通過標準如下：

III. 成績計算及通過標準

初　試	通過標準 / 滿分	複　試	通過標準 / 滿分
聽力測驗 閱讀能力測驗 寫作能力測驗	80 / 120 分 80 / 120 分 70 / 100 分	口說能力測驗	80 / 100 分

IV. 寫作能力測驗級分說明

第一部份：單句寫作級分說明

級　分	說　　明
2	正確無誤。
1	有誤，但重點結構正確。
0	錯誤過多、未答、等同未答。

第二部份：段落寫作級分說明

級　分	說　　明
5	正確表達題目之要求；文法、用字等幾乎無誤。
4	大致正確表達題目之要求；文法、用字等有誤，但不影響讀者之理解。
3	大致回答題目之要求，但未能完全達意；文法、用字等有誤，稍影響讀者之理解。
2	部份回答題目之要求，表達上有令人不解/誤解之處；文法、用字等皆有誤，讀者須耐心解讀。
1	僅回答1個問題或重點；文法、用字等錯誤過多，嚴重影響讀者之理解。
0	未答、等同未答。

各部份題型之題數、級分及總分計算公式：

分項測驗	測驗題型	各部份題數	每題級分	佔總分比重
第一部份：單句寫作	A. 句子改寫	5題	2分	50 %
	B. 句子合併	5題	2分	
	C. 重組	5題	2分	
第二部份：段落寫作	看圖表寫作	1篇	5分	50 %
總分計算公式	公式：{(第一部份得分/30) + (第二部份得分/5)}×50 例：第一部份各項得分 A－8分 　　　　　　　　　　　B－10分 　　　　　　　　　　　C－8分 8+10+8=26 三項加總第一部份得分 － 26分 第二部份得分 － 4分 依公式計算如下： {(26/30) + (4/5)}×50=83　該考生得分83分			

　　凡應考且合乎規定者一律發給成績單。初試及複試各項測驗成績通過者，發給合格證書，本測驗成績紀錄保存兩年。

　　初試通過者，可於一年內單獨報考複試，得重複報考。惟複試一旦通過，即不得再報考。

　　已通過本英檢測驗初級，一年內不得再報考同級數之測驗。違反本規定報考者，其應試資格將被取消，且不退費。

（以上資料取自「全民英檢學習網站」http://www.gept.org.tw）

劉毅英文初級英檢模考班

I. **上課時間：** 每週日下午 2：00～5：00

II. **上課方式：** 完全比照財團法人語言訓練中心所做「初級英語檢定測驗」初
試標準。分為聽力測驗、閱讀能力測驗、及寫作能力測驗三部
分。每次上課舉行 70 分鐘的模擬考，包含 30 題聽力測驗，35
題詞彙結構、段落填空、閱讀理解、及 16 題單句寫作、及一篇
段落寫作。考完試後立即講解，馬上釐清所有問題。

III. **收費標準：** （含代辦初級檢定考試報名及簡章費用）

期　　數	3個月	6個月	1年保證班
週　　數	12週	24週	48週
費　　用	5800元	9800元	14800元

※ 1. 劉毅英文同學優待 *1000* 元。

　 2. 保證班若無通過，免費贈送一年課程。

IV. **報名贈書：** 初級英檢全套書籍

報名立刻開始背誦「初級英檢公佈字彙①－⑩」

劉毅英文・毅志文理補習班（兒美、國中、高中、成人班、全民英檢代辦報名）

班址：台北市許昌街 17 號 6 F（火車站前・壽德大樓）　☎（02）2389-5212

||||||||||||||| ● 學習出版公司門市部 ● |||||||||||||||

台北地區：台北市許昌街 10 號 2 樓 TEL：(02)2331-4060・2331-9209
台中地區：台中市綠川東街 32 號 8 樓 23 室
　　　　　TEL：(04)2223-2838

||||||||||||||||||||||||||||||||||||||||||||||

初級英語聽力檢定⑥

主　　　編／劉　毅
發　行　所／學習出版有限公司　　　　　☎ (02) 2704-5525
郵　撥　帳　號／0512727-2 學習出版社帳戶
登　記　證／局版台業 2179 號
印　刷　所／裕強彩色印刷有限公司
台 北 門 市／台北市許昌街 10 號 2 F　　☎ (02) 2331-4060・2331-9209
台 中 門 市／台中市綠川東街 32 號 8 F 23 室　☎ (04) 2223-2838
台灣總經銷／紅螞蟻圖書有限公司　　　☎ (02) 2799-9490・2657-0132
美國總經銷／Evergreen Book Store　　☎ (818) 2813622

售價：新台幣一百八十元正

2006 年 1 月 1 日初版

ISBN 957-519-841-7
版權所有・翻印必究